SUMMER AT THE COSY COTTAGE CAFE

A FEEL-GOOD SECOND-CHANCE ROMANCE

RACHEL GRIFFITHS

For my family,
you are my inspiration and my world.

SUMMER AT THE COSY COTTAGE CAFÉ

By Rachel Griffiths

Allie Jones loves her cosy cottage café in the picturesque village of Heatherlea. She has her independence, two grown-up children and two cute cats. Life is settled and she thinks she's happy.

Author Chris Monroe has it all. Critical success, a luxurious London apartment, and the kind of jet-set lifestyle most people dream of. But something's missing.

When a family bereavement throws these two old friends together, they begin to question the true meaning of happiness.

Love is in the air, but do Allie and Chris have room in their hands-on lives for more than a summer fling?

Edited by: Kerry Barrett

Cover design by: Emma L.J. Byrne

1

"Such a terrible loss, Mrs Burnley. I really am sorry."

Allie Jones nodded solemnly as the elderly woman dabbed at her eyes with a tissue.

"She was a good friend… all these years." Judith Burnley's watery eyes burned into Allie's. "Since school you know? Even though she was a few years older than me, we were still so close."

"I can't imagine how you must be feeling."

"Dreadful. *Dreadful.*" Mrs Burnley's emphasis caused a tiny bead of saliva to land on her chin. "I still can't believe she's gone. Although it was a lovely service."

"Oh good. I would have gone myself but I had to be here to get everything ready."

"Of course you did. Her son said some very nice things about her. He's a good lad that Chris Monroe."

"Yes, indeed."

Allie chewed her bottom lip, wondering how long she was supposed to stand with the older woman. After all, what length of time did social etiquette demand? Plus, she really didn't want to discuss Chris right now and had been trying not to think about him too much.

"I hope someone says positive things about me at my funeral. At my age, I probably don't have much time left…"

Time!

The word made Allie think about the miniature quiches in the oven. She needed to rescue them. Five more minutes would mean perfect pastry but any longer and they'd be ruined.

"I'm sorry, but I need to get back to the kitchen. I have a thousand things to do before everyone arrives."

Mrs Burnley's grey eyebrows shot up her heavily powdered forehead.

"I have quiches in the oven that will burn," Allie added, in case the urgency of the situation was in any doubt. She placed a hand on the older woman's arm. "Again, I'm sorry."

Mrs Burnley seemed placated. She gave a sharp sniff then headed across the café to a group of women standing near the log burner. Their uniform of black skirts and jackets paired with flesh-coloured tights, made Allie think of a nature documentary she'd once seen about crows, especially as they took it in turns to cast inquisitive glances around the café.

Allie picked up two used cups from a table near the counter then went through to the kitchen. The quiches should have been ready before the funeral party started arriving. She was sure the service had been scheduled for eleven o'clock and hadn't expected anyone to turn up at the café until around noon. But the group of women had arrived promptly at eleven thirty-five, so Allie guessed they had left the small village church as soon as the final hymn had been sung.

Poor Chris!

Allie hadn't seen Chris Monroe in years. After he'd left the village, he rarely returned. Allie thought she had an idea why, having known his mother – the rather harsh Mrs Monroe – since she was a child, but there could be other reasons she knew nothing about. Whenever she'd asked Mrs Monroe how Chris was getting on, her stock response had been 'he's travelling with his writing' and that was as much as Allie had known. Until a week ago, when she'd received a phone call out of the blue, from Chris himself.

The call had been polite and brief, not allowing for more detailed pleasantries or a potted history. In fact, if Allie was being honest, Chris had been a bit rude and rather cold. But business was business and she wasn't going to turn down a job. Besides, where else would they have held the wake? At one of the village pubs? Allie knew that Mrs Monroe would never have been happy with that. The old woman had seen the local pubs as dens of iniquity and would, no doubt, have turned in her new grave had her son chosen to hold her wake surrounded by locals enjoying a lunchtime pint.

Allie shivered. All this thinking about graves and funerals summoned her own dark clouds to the horizon and the old sadness tugged at her heart. She didn't have time for this today, so she'd have to pin her knickers to her vest and get on with things.

She opened the oven door and the comforting aromas of grilled cheese and caramelised onion greeted her. *Just in time!* She removed the trays from the oven then set them on the worktop to cool.

"Hey, Mum!"

Allie turned to find Jordan had joined her in the kitchen.

3

"Oh thank goodness! I thought you'd forgotten you were working this morning."

He shook his head and his floppy fringe fell over his left eye.

"Of course not. Would I let you down?" He gave her a cheeky grin then pulled an apron from a drawer and hooped it over his head. Allie knew she could tell her son that he had let her down in the past, and that, yes, he did sometimes oversleep and forget about his Saturday morning shifts at the café too, but she didn't. He was here now and that was what mattered.

"Where do you want me?"

"You oversee things out front. I'll get everything finished up in here then come and help you. Just keep the tea and coffee going."

Jordan paused then rubbed the back of his neck as he inhaled deeply, a sign that he was worrying about something.

"What is it, love?"

"Mum… Are you, uh, okay?"

"Why, Jordan?"

He met her eyes and she watched as he chewed his lower lip.

"Well, you know, with this being a wake."

Allie nodded. "Honestly, I'm fine. This isn't the first wake we've done since your dad…" She swallowed the end of her sentence.

"Well I'm here for you."

"I know and I'm here for you too. I love you, Jordan."

He smiled. "I know."

"Now go and make some hot beverages."

"Yes ma'am!"

He gave her a mock salute then disappeared.

Allie knew why he was concerned about her and she

worried about him for the same reason. Funerals always reminded them of Roger's and although she had been strong in front of her children at the time, it had been truly awful.

She turned her attention back to the quiches and removed them from the trays, then deposited them onto foil serving platters before adding sprigs of decorative parsley. The pastry was light and crisp and the cheese on top had a rich golden hue. She might have got some things wrong in her life but she did know how to bake, and opening the café had been, perhaps, the best decision she'd ever made. Of course, it had been a lifelong ambition too, one she'd harboured since her days at secondary school when she'd excelled at food technology. She'd always enjoyed baking with her mother as a child and an enthusiastic cookery teacher had encouraged her to consider baking as a career.

However, she'd fallen in love after while sitting her A Levels and an unexpected pregnancy had led her to sideline her ambitions. She'd still baked regularly and taken cakes and savoury delights to birthday parties, village fetes and church celebrations, but thought her café dreams would never be realised. Some things brought out a wave of yearning in her, like occasional trips to Bath when they'd visit the delightful tearooms for refreshments, but she'd told herself she was lucky to be a wife and mother and tucked her old ambitions firmly away.

Until her life had changed dramatically and she'd had to make some big decisions.

Allie shook the sadness away; she couldn't afford to think about all that right now. She had to focus on the positives. She'd had another good spring, and early summer was looking good so far – in part because the medieval Surrey village of Heatherlea was a tourist attraction, which meant plenty of business for the café—and she was seeing some pleasing profits. Her situation was looking better by the minute and she was hoping that August would bring plenty of customers. She had her own business, two wonderful grown-up children, two funny cats and her grief was not as sharp as it once was.

She crossed her fingers instinctively as superstition shrouded her. The future looked bright but she'd never take anything for granted. Everything could change within minutes.

She lifted two of the serving platters of quiches and turned round to take them through to the café, then let out a screech as she hit a wall of chest. Quiches and parsley went flying into the air and the platters crashed to the floor. Allie was only saved from face planting into cheesy pastry by two strong hands that caught her, just in time.

"Allie, I'm so sorry!"

She shook her head and a chunk of quiche dropped onto her shoulder then bounced off and landed on the tiles.

"Chris?"

"Yes."

His dark eyes roamed her face, familiar yet different. Older. Wiser.

"What on earth were you doing sneaking around like that?"

She realised that he was still supporting her, so she took a step backwards and slipped out of his grasp.

He looked at his hands, as if surprised that they'd been wedged under her armpits, then back at her face.

"The um… the young man out front told me you were in here and I came to check that everything was okay."

"Yes, everything's fine. Well, it was fine until you just…" She swallowed the rest of her sentence, not wanting to accuse him of quiche destruction on what must be a very difficult day. Then she realised he was staring hard at her. Heat rushed into her cheeks, so she broke eye contact and picked at a bit of onion that was stuck to the neckline of her good white blouse – the one she wore for funerals and wakes. "And that was my son, Jordan."

Chris ran a hand through his salt-and-pepper hair and sighed as if exhausted. His face was still handsome but he had tiny lines engraved around his eyes, suggesting that he frowned or squinted a lot. The last time Allie had seen him, his hair had been black as a raven's wing, but that had been about ten years ago. And then she'd only seen him in passing. Apart from the recent phone call, she hadn't spoken to him in over twenty years – not since her wedding reception. When she'd returned from her honeymoon in Tenby, Chris had already left Heatherlea, leaving no details for her or Roger to contact him. She'd tried to talk to her husband about it but he'd always found a way to avoid the conversation, as if the friendship they'd once had with Chris was something she'd imagined. And she hadn't liked to keep pushing, because even Chris's name seemed to irritate Roger and she'd hated to upset him. His moods had been so unpredictable.

"Again, I am sorry. I'm running a bit later than expected because I went to the cemetery, but then everything got a bit delayed because the vicar got his foot stuck in the freshly dug earth at the graveside and lost his shoe. It took three people to pull it out and by that time he'd stumbled and got his sock all wet and it was just…" He rubbed his eyes. "Anyway, I came to say hello and it was so weird when I saw you stood there. You look exactly the same as you did at eighteen."

Allie laughed. "I doubt that." She swallowed her retort about a fatter bottom and thicker waistline. "But thank you. You don't look that different either."

"Except for the rugged grooves on my face and the George Clooney hair, right?"

"Mum!" Jordan interrupted as he appeared in the doorway. "They're all arriving."

"Okay, I'll be there in a moment." She scanned the floor with dismay; it was clear that none of the mini quiches she'd dropped were salvageable. Thankfully, she had two more foil platters on the work surface and another batch in the freezer that she could pop in the oven.

"Is there anything I can do to help?" Chris gestured at the quiche carnage.

"No. Thank you. You have to be out there with the… uh… guests. I'll sort this out."

"Thanks. Catch up later?" He looked at her from under his dark lashes, as if suddenly shy.

"Yes. Sure. That would be nice."

Chris left the kitchen and Allie located the dustpan and brush.

As she started to sweep up the mess, she wondered at the way her heart was thumping behind her ribs. Had Chris really startled her that much, or was there something else about seeing him that had made her heart beat faster?

Allie stood behind the counter and surveyed the funeral party in her café. The crows had taken themselves to a table by the window and were tucking into sandwiches and fruitcake. She watched as Jordan approached them with the large stainless steel teapot, and filled each cup in turn. The elderly women were certainly making the most of Mrs Monroe's wake and Mrs Burnley had a big smile on her face, as if her sadness about her friend had already receded. But perhaps she was just reminiscing. It was better to try to remember the good times when you lost someone you cared about; Allie knew that better than most. And she also knew that keeping busy was the best way to avoid dwelling on the past.

She carried a tray of vanilla-frosted cupcakes around, offering them to people she knew and strangers alike, until the tray was empty and her face ached from maintaining a polite smile and repeating words of condolence.

Every time Allie attended a funeral and a wake, she had to battle her own demons, but she suspected it was that way for most people. The grief of others was bound to remind you of your own. Although it was true, the old adage, that time did help with the healing process. The pain would never completely disappear, but it wasn't quite as sharp, except for those odd occasions when it took her by surprise. But that was to be expected; she had lost her husband, after all, and when he was so young.

She swallowed hard. Roger had been gone six years and she had kept going by putting one foot in front of the other. That was how it was done. Some days were harder than others and she couldn't deny that she sometimes indulged in daydreams about what might have been had things worked out differently, but she had become quite adept at giving herself a firm shake and donning the good old stiff upper lip. Besides, her version of *differently* was more complicated than she cared to admit to herself.

It wasn't until after everyone had gone and she was filling the dishwasher that she realised she hadn't seen Chris again.

"Jordan?"

Her son paused in covering sausage rolls with cling film. "Yeah?"

"Did you see Mr Monroe at all?"

"Why, Mum? Has he done a runner without paying you?" He waggled his eyebrows at her.

"No. Uh… I don't think so anyway."

Chris had paid a deposit over the phone when he'd booked the café but she hadn't seen him to take the balance. Although in circumstances like these, she often didn't expect the rest on the actual day because people were generally too upset to think about money. Her daughter, Mandy, told her she was too soft and that she let people take advantage, but Allie saw it as part of what The Cosy Cottage Café represented for her and for the locals. It wasn't all about the money and she could trust most people to pay her within a few days. Chris would likely do the same.

"I just didn't see him again after he… popped into the kitchen to say hello and I wondered if he was okay."

Jordan scrunched up his nose then flicked his head to clear his fringe out of his eyes. He had, thankfully, worn a clip in it for most of the day – to avoid adding his blond hairs to the food he was serving – but it seemed that he'd removed it since the café had emptied. Which meant the leftover sausage rolls would now have to be eaten by Allie, Jordan and the cats. *Just in case.*

"He's probably just upset, Mum. He has lost his mother. Perhaps he went out for some fresh air. I'm sure he'll be back tomorrow."

"Yes. I'm sure you're right."

Allie closed the dishwasher then switched it on and went to the sink to wash her hands. She gazed out of the latticed kitchen window at the pergola she'd had built in the spring, where the fragrant pink flowers of the climbing honeysuckle now bloomed in abundance. As well as being good at baking, she'd discovered that she had green fingers, and everything she'd planted within the café garden was thriving. There was a definite satisfaction to be found in gardening and enjoying the fruits of that pastime.

She went through to the café and made a mug of tea, then took it over to the comfy leather sofa in the corner by the window. She put the mug on the small wooden table then slumped onto the sofa and smiled as it squished up around her. It was an old one that she'd found in a charity shop and it was exactly what she'd imagined having in her own café. Behind it, and on the opposite wall, were shelves full of books all genres. Her regulars often brought in books they'd read and donated them to her shelves then took ones that they wanted to read. On quieter days, and sometimes after closing, Allie liked to curl up on the sofa with a warm drink and a book and to lose herself in another world.

The café was, in her eyes, perfect. Inside and out. The exterior was chocolate-box pretty with a thatched roof and shuttered windows. Roses climbed around the door and ivy climbed the walls. A café sign in the shape of a teapot hung from the side of the building. She had sown wild-flower seeds for the bees and butterflies in pots and raised beds, and as it was summer, everything in the garden was in full bloom. She'd even managed to find some colourful milk-urn planters that she'd filled with trailing nasturtiums and their bright orange, red and gold flowers made her heart lift every time she saw them.

Inside, she'd had the two front rooms of the cottage converted into one big room, with the counter in the far right corner from the door and the café kitchen behind that. Allie had gone for the shabby-chic look, using reclaimed wood and second-hand furniture that she found online and in antique shops, and tables in a variety of colours and shapes took up most of the floor space. She often wondered if it was a reaction to the life she'd shared with Roger, when everything from their house to their carpets to their towels had to be brand new, spick and span. After he had died, Allie had gone out of her way to find the perfect old cottage to convert into a café, as well as searching for the loveliest second-hand furniture, fixtures and fittings. Roger had wanted everything in his home to tell people how successful he was and how well he was doing. And for a while, Allie had gone along with that, but when she'd lost the first flush of youth and Roger had expressed his disappointment with that, Allie had been devastated. So yes, perhaps her rebellion against all things new was deliberate.

A large log burner was centred on the back wall, directly opposite the front door. It wasn't currently lit but had logs piled up inside it with sprigs of dried lavender and rosemary tucked in around them. On cold winter days, the log burner kept the café warm and the table nearest to it was very popular.

The ceiling was white with exposed wooden beams that gave the café the cosy cottage atmosphere Allie had envisioned. She'd hung salvaged 1920s raspberry glass pendant lights from between the beams and they created a relaxing ambience in the darker afternoons that came with autumn and winter.

As she sipped her tea, the strains of being on her feet all day slipped away, and her thoughts strayed once more to Chris. It wasn't the money she was worried about, and she had no doubts that he would pay his bill. She just really wanted to see him again. He was one of her oldest friends and she'd like to catch up and find out how he'd been all these years. Everyone of her own age in the village seemed to be married or remarried, and lots of her old school friends had moved away a long time ago.

At one point Allie, Roger and Chris had been inseparable. A wave of nostalgia washed over her and she shuddered with surprise. Chris's return to Heatherlea was having quite an impact on her.

She did have some good friends in the village now; they just weren't ones she'd grown up with. So it would be nice if she got the chance to chat to Chris about old times. And there was nothing wrong in wanting to do that with an old friend now, was there?

*A*llie peered at the red digital display of the clock on the bedside table and groaned. It was six o'clock but her room was still quite dark and that never inspired her to get out of bed.

She rolled over and was greeted by a terrible stench.

"Eurgh!" She reached out and her hand met soft warm fur. "Is that you, Ebony?"

The cat purred in response.

"Where's your sister?"

As if summoned, silver grey Luna pushed open Allie's bedroom door and entered, bringing a warm glow from the hallway. Jordan must have forgotten to turn the light off again before he went to sleep.

Allie sat up and swung her legs over the edge of the bed. The double bed that she usually shared with a cat. While Luna was quite an independent feline, preferring to spend her nights going in and out of the cat flap on the backdoor, Ebony liked to spend her nights cuddled up to her mistress. Although Allie had originally tried to discourage the cat from sleeping with her, she now welcomed the presence of another living being at night. It could get lonely and Ebony offered the sweet, unassuming company that Allie appreciated.

Luna let out a meow then began circling Allie's legs.

"I know, I know. Time for some breakfast."

Both cats shot out of the bedroom door and Allie followed them, pulling on her dressing gown as she descended the stairs.

After she bought the cottage, she'd had a ground-floor extension built at the rear. The building maintained its original façade but out back was an L shape, with her kitchen and lounge overlooking the back garden. When she'd had the property renovated, turning the ground floor into The Cosy Cottage Café, she'd kept the first floor as it was, with three bedrooms. Two of the bedrooms were small but the master bedroom was an adequate double. The bathroom, however, was the size of a phone box with just a shower, sink and toilet, and Allie did sometimes miss soaking in a bubble bath. But she couldn't deny that it was cosy and she was perfectly comfortable there.

The cottage offered the security she'd craved following the loss of her husband, and Allie, Jordan and the cats managed just fine. She did miss Mandy, who had moved away to attend university just before Roger died, and only ever returned for a few days at a time. However, she understood that her daughter was following her dream career in publishing and that she had to be at the heart of it all in London. Besides, Allie knew that Mandy had struggled terribly with the loss of her father, and that coming back to Heatherlea was painful for her. So she kept a room ready for Mandy, in case she ever wanted to come home, but she suspected that her daughter never would, at least not on a permanent basis.

Allie switched the kettle on then poured cat kibble into

two bowls under the breakfast bar. As the cats crunched contentedly, she made herself a mug of tea and drank it gazing out of the long windows that overlooked her lush green garden and the fields beyond, watching as the sky changed from indigo to rose. The old saying *red sky at morning, shepherd's warning...* popped into her mind. She really hoped it wouldn't rain today because she had washing to peg on the line, including the tablecloths from the wake yesterday, and she wanted to try to get out for a walk. It was all very well owning a café and being able to bake delicious delights for her customers, but Allie sometimes enjoyed a few too many of those delights herself, from leftover cupcakes with rich fondant icing to buttery croissants that melted in the mouth, to tasty savoury quiches. So she tried to walk every day to keep the wobbles at bay.

Chris certainly hadn't looked like he had any extra pounds to spare, even though he must be forty-four now, at two years older than Allie. In fact, he looked pretty good with his salt-and-pepper hair and lean jaw, as if time had improved him like a fine wine. And his chocolate-brown eyes were still gorgeous. She recalled how they used to twinkle mischievously, suggesting that he knew far more about what she was thinking than she could ever imagine. But that had been before everything had changed.

"Mum!" Allie jumped and spilt tea down her fluffy dressing gown. "Where are the frosted flakes?"

"When did you get up, Jordan?"

"Just now."

"But it's not even seven o'clock yet." He wasn't an early riser, even as a child at Christmas time when Allie had been up hours before him and Mandy, waiting for them to wake up and open their presents. And waiting for Roger to wake up, of course, because Christmas Eve often saw him enjoying a few drinks at the pub then not wanting to rise too early the following day.

"My rumbling stomach woke me."

"Oh." Allie grabbed a tea towel and tried to use it to mop some of the tea from her front. "Didn't you eat enough yesterday?"

He shrugged.

"Maybe not. Anyway, what's got you gazing into the distance?"

"What?"

He produced a box of cereal from the cupboard then shook it.

"Your face was all dreamy like you were thinking about what you'd do with a lottery win."

"Was it?" Allie shook her head then pointed at the fridge where a magnetic notepad held the weekly shopping list. "Write frosted flakes on there."

He nodded then peered into the cereal box. "Not sure these bran flakes are still good. They look a bit grey."

"Toast?"

"Please."

Allie opened the bread bin and pulled out a wholemeal loaf then popped a few slices into the toaster. Thank goodness Jordan thought she was daydreaming about the lottery. If he knew the truth, she suspected he'd be horrified. Allie was way past the stage where she fantasised about handsome men and way past the stage where she could imagine being with anyone again.

Besides, Chris was just an old friend and she doubted he'd be hanging around in Heatherlea for long. So she'd have to make sure she didn't allow her fantasies to get too carried away.

"Ooh! What's happened to you?" Camilla Dix leaned on the counter and stared hard.

Heat rushed into Allie's cheeks at the sudden scrutiny.

"What do you mean?"

"Well," Camilla narrowed her eyes, "you look different."

"Do I?" Allie turned to the counter behind her and picked up a plate laden with sandwiches.

She pretended to arrange the triangular slices of bread for a moment, so her colour would have time to fade. When she turned back to her friend, Camilla had her hands on her hips and was chewing her bottom lip. "I know what it is!"

"Oh?" Allie came from behind the counter and carried the plate of sandwiches to the table in front of the log burner. She put it down then busied herself setting four places with cutlery and wine glasses.

Camilla clapped her hands. "You're wearing makeup!"

Allie frowned. "So? I always wear makeup."

"No you don't."

"I do, just not much."

"It's the mascara and flicky eyeliner." Camilla gestured with her hands in a manner that suggested Allie had wings either side of her nose.

Allie shrugged. "Just trying something new."

"It looks nice."

"Thanks."

The door to the café opened and two women entered.

"Hello!" Camilla's younger sister, Dawn Dix-Beaumont crossed to Allie and hugged her then did the same to Camilla. "Feels like a year since we last got together. It has been *such* a long week." She pulled out a chair and sat down.

"Allie, it smells incredible in here. Have you made lemon drizzle cake?" Honey Blackwell sniffed the air dramatically and Allie smiled. Honey was currently enthused about an amateur dramatics class that she was taking and everything she did was exaggerated, as if to show how good she was at acting.

"I know it's your favourite, Honey." Allie said. "I'll just get the wine."

She went through to the kitchen and got two bottles of white from the wine cooler. When she returned to the café, she paused for a moment by the counter and smiled. Six years ago, her life was very different; she had a husband and two children and lived in what was then a new-build on the other side of the village. Her daily routine had involved household chores and a certain amount of daytime TV. She'd been plodding along, even though she'd sensed that something wasn't quite right, possibly that something was missing. Of course, her daughter had gone off to university, leaving her with the beginnings of empty-nest syndrome. But at least she'd still had Jordan at home – leaving his dirty socks lying around, as well as plenty of dirty dishes in the sink and muddy shoes in the hallway.

Then everything had changed.

She'd lost Roger, twice in one day. *Out of the blue.* Well, she'd told herself it had been out of the blue but she sometimes suspected that she'd known more than she'd cared to admit to herself. The accident had been fast and fatal, tearing Roger from his family forever. Allie had been left to pick up the pieces.

And now…

She'd used his significant life insurance to invest in a fresh start. It had been hard at first, because she'd found that she didn't want to touch the money, almost as if it was tainted. But necessity had driven her to see a financial adviser and to consider her future, as well as that of her children.

She had never really liked the new-build, preferring the quirks and idiosyncrasies of older cottages, as well as having her view of it distorted by Roger's obsession with everything new – including women, it later emerged – so selling the family home hadn't been that hard. Then she'd put an offer in on the rather run-down cottage and with the help of a good local builder, had transformed it into The Cosy Cottage Café. The necessary food hygiene qualifications had been acquired while the building work was being done, and Allie had worked hard to bring everything together.

With the passing of time, had come new friendships. The raven-haired, green-eyed sisters Camilla and Dawn had always lived in the village, but with them being younger than Allie, at seven and nine years respectively, she'd only ever known them to say hello to in passing. Then one day they'd come into the café together on a quiet day, and Allie had ended up joining them for a coffee. And that had been that. As for hippy Honey, as Allie affectionately thought of her sweet-natured friend, the twenty-six year old artist had inherited her aunt's cottage in Heatherlea two years ago, and soon settled into a routine as one of their group. With her light-brown eyes and green and blue hair that made Allie think of a mermaid, she always brought a smile to Allie's face. She was only two years older than Mandy, but very different to Allie's serious daughter, and Allie sometimes wondered if the young women would get on should they meet.

She suspected that Mandy's grief had affected her deeply and added to her serious nature, but also knew that growing up with a father like Roger would have had an impact upon her. He had loved his children and provided for them, but he'd been so stern and such a perfectionist, and it had been hard to live up to what he'd expected from his family. Allie knew she could have made the move to leave him when Mandy and Jordan were younger but she hadn't been able to bring herself to do it. Roger's parents had both died when he was at university – his mother first then his father two years later – so she'd worried about him being alone. Her own parents had always been so happy and united, and Allie believed in marriage and commitment. As soon as she'd known she was carrying Mandy, she'd felt that she had only one course open to her: marriage to Roger, and he had agreed wholeheartedly. She didn't want her parents to see her as a failure, as being incapable of finding the love they shared. Even though she knew they'd never express it outwardly, the idea that they might think it made her sad, especially as she felt she'd let them down by not going on to higher education as she'd planned. She hadn't wanted to fail at that, then at her marriage. So she'd stuck with Roger in spite of her misgivings.

But times had changed. Allie didn't know how she'd manage without her Tuesday evenings at the café. They were her weekly highlight. She'd shut up shop at five-thirty, then Camilla, Dawn and Honey would arrive and they'd put the world to rights over wine, sandwiches, savoury pastries and cake. And often more wine. They could have gone through to her personal kitchen and lounge, but the café was so cosy, especially on chilly autumnal evenings, that they had automatically gathered around the log burner instead.

"What do you think?" Camilla asked loudly, dragging

Allie back to the present, and all three turned to look at her.

"Ooh, suits you!" Honey said. "Very pretty."

Dawn nodded.

"I like it. What's the occasion?"

Allie took the wine to the table and opened a bottle then filled their glasses in turn.

"There's no occasion, I just wanted to try wearing my makeup differently."

When all glasses were filled, Allie sat down next to Camilla then raised her wine.

"To Tuesday evenings!"

Her friends raised their glasses and clinked them against Allie's.

Suddenly, Dawn coughed and spat a mouthful of wine back into her glass.

"God what's wrong?" Allie asked. "Don't you like it?"

Dawn shook her head.

"You want red?" Camilla asked.

Dawn shook her head again then her face crumpled.

"Oh, sweetheart." Allie got up and went round the table to hug her friend. "It's okay if you don't like it. Not everyone's a fan of Pinot Grigio."

Dawn waved a hand.

"It's not that. I do like the wine and I wish I could drink it but I can't…" A tear trickled down her face, so Allie rubbed her back in the same way she used to do the children's when they had fallen over and hurt themselves.

Camilla shook her head and mouthed *no idea* at Allie and Honey.

When Dawn finally stopped sobbing, Allie smoothed her friend's dark hair back from her forehead and handed her a tissue.

"You want to talk about it? Then we're here. You don't? At least get some food into you. You're probably just exhausted running round after two kids and a husband. I know what it's like; I've been there remember."

Camilla shuddered.

"Can't think of anything worse." Then she held up her hands. "Not that I don't adore my niece and nephew but it's a lot to deal with on a daily basis. I'm full of admiration for you, little sister."

"It's not that either. I am tired, yes, but it's something else."

Allie looked around the table at her friends then gave Dawn another hug.

"Ah… I think I know."

"You do?"

"Well I don't think you're crying because you've got a water infection and are on antibiotics and can't drink alcohol. So are you—"

"Yes." Dawn sniffed. "Somehow, in spite of using bloody condoms and being on the pill, we've managed to get pregnant again. Just when I was starting to feel normal. When I've finally got James sleeping through at night." She blew her nose loudly.

Camilla took a gulp of wine then raised her glass.

"I guess here's where we say congratulations."

"You just said you couldn't imagine anything worse than having children." Dawn scrunched the tissue up as she stared at her sister.

"Yes but you're a great mum and one more won't make a massive difference will it?"

"I guess not. I hope not."

"And we'll all be here for you," Allie added.

"Sorry am I intruding?"

Allie turned to see Chris standing in the doorway. She hadn't even heard him come in. Her heart skipped as she took in his faded jeans, navy hoodie and scuffed brown boots. The shadow of stubble on his chin matched his hair colour and somehow his eyes seemed darker than yesterday.

"No!" She released Dawn then smoothed her hair. "Not at all."

"Hi." Chris waved at the other women then came closer. "I need to pay for the wake. I meant to do it yesterday but the day got away from me, then I had a few things to deal with this morning and before I knew it…" He held out his hands.

"Better late than never," Allie said, offering what she hoped was a warm smile.

They crossed to the counter and she went behind it to locate the bill.

"Here you are." She waited as he perused it. "Is it okay? No nasty surprises?" Behind him, Camilla was grinning at her and Honey was making heart signs with her thumbs and forefingers. None of them had attended the funeral, as they hadn't known Mrs Monroe very well, and as far as Allie knew, they hadn't met Chris before.

"No problem at all. It's very reasonable." He glanced behind him and Honey and Camilla quickly stopped what they were doing and feigned interest in their food. "I just… uh… I wondered if you might like to catch up sometime." He raised his eyebrows then pulled a credit card from his wallet and handed it to her.

"Oh!" She held the card for a minute then realised she was supposed to put it through the card machine. "If you'll just input your pin, please."

Chris typed in four numbers and the machine beeped.

"You can take your card back now." Allie handed him a receipt then put the transaction through the till.

"So what do you think?"

"About catching up?" Her chest had tightened and her neck felt stiff and twitchy. This was ridiculous. He was an old friend asking her if she wanted to catch up, not if she wanted to jump into bed with him. But he was so handsome and Allie didn't have much interaction with the opposite sex, except to serve them food and drink in the café and even then a lot of them were over sixty and accompanied by their wives.

"Yes. We could go for a drink. Perhaps Friday? I would've suggested tomorrow but you're probably busy."

Allie wasn't busy but rational thought seemed to have deserted her. Besides, she realised that she needed some time to mentally prepare herself before 'catching up' with Chris.

"Friday would be lovely. We could go to The Red Fox, if you like? They serve great bar meals."

"Brilliant. Shall I pick you up or meet you there?"

Allie imagined Jordan's reaction if she was collected by a man from their home. Her son might be twenty-three but he was still so young in some ways and she didn't want to worry him. Better if he didn't know too much about this. She was just going for a meal with an old friend, after all.

"Meet me there? I'll have to tidy up after closing anyway and sort out Jordan's tea." Jordan was capable of making his own meals but she didn't want to have to rush to get ready.

"Okay, no problem. See you there about seven-thirty then?"

"Great."

Chris paused for moment as if wanting to say more,

but he glanced at the three women again, then gave a small shake of his head. "Bye then, Allie."

"Bye."

"Bye ladies."

"Byeeee!" they cooed.

Allie watched as the door closed behind him then returned to her seat.

"*Who* was that?" Camilla demanded.

"Just an old friend." Allie took a sip of her wine.

"He seems familiar."

"He's an author. You've probably seen his picture on the back of a book cover or something. He's in Heatherlea because his mother passed away and I catered the wake yesterday."

"Ahhhh." Camilla nodded.

"Anyway, how're you feeling now, Dawn?"

Dawn shook her head. "Never mind me, Allie Jones. Did I hear you agree to go out on a date?"

"She did!" Camilla said. "In all the time we've been friends, no men around. Not one. Then out of the blue, George Clooney's double appears."

Allie laughed. "Hardly. He's at least ten years younger."

"Even better!" Dawn said, rubbing her hands together. "Now then, how about you tell us all about Mr Clooney-come-author?" She picked up her wine glass and raised it to her lips then slammed it back down on the table again. "Dammit!"

"I'll get you some orange juice." Allie got up and went to the fridge behind the counter.

"And when you sit back down you're telling us every-thing." Camilla thumped the table.

Allie knew she had no choice but to give her friends some background information. She'd never spoken about

Chris because it was… complicated, and not the type of thing you randomly threw into conversation. It was almost as if she'd separated her life into two sections: before and after the café.

Camilla topped up her glass. "I think you're going to need this."

"I think you're right," Allie said. She took a big swig of wine then swallowed it. "So, to begin at the beginning…"

3

_T_he following three days passed in a blur of opening the café, baking, exchanging pleasantries with customers and cleaning up after closing. But when Friday morning arrived, Allie was a bag of nerves. Which was ridiculous really, seeing as how she wasn't even going on a date, just meeting an old friend for a drink.

At four-thirty, she was browsing cake recipes on her tablet, trying not to think about how she would feel being alone with Chris again, when the door to the café opened and Camilla sashayed in.

"What are you doing here? Shouldn't you be working?"

Camilla smiled. "It's a beautifully sunny Friday afternoon, so I finished a bit early. I had a lunchtime appointment with a client in London then I deliberately kept the rest of the day free."

"Why? Are you going somewhere?" Allie asked the question though she already had her suspicions about why Camilla might have come to see her.

"Yes. I'm going to ensure that you're ready for your date."

"Oh Camilla, it's not a date! How many times?" Allie sighed with exasperation. Her three friends had bombarded her with texts and social media messages about her so called 'date' since Tuesday. At first, it had amused her and she'd glanced at them then got on with what she was doing, but by this morning, it had started to add to her anxiety about the evening.

Camilla placed her bag on the counter and shrugged out of her olive-green linen jacket. "Allie, we only want to see you happy."

"I am happy."

"You are… I guess… but we want to see you happier."

"Why do I need a man to be *happier*?" Allie realised she'd raised her voice when the two women sat at the window table turned to look at her. She smiled at them. "You're single, Camilla and I don't see you looking for love."

Camilla shook her head. "I'm not looking for anything, darling. But I do have male *friends*."

"Your one night stands that Dawn's always fretting about?"

"Look, none of the men I see are unvetted and they're all in the same boat as me; they don't want a committed relationship and neither do I. So we, you know… enjoy each other's company. And just because Dawnie is happily married, doesn't mean I have to be."

Allie bit back her reply. Camilla had never been in a relationship that she knew of but she seemed at peace with that. And Allie could understand why she was happy with life being that way: Camilla was a freelance accountant, she had plenty of clients – including Allie – and when she wanted some male company, she had no shortage of admirers. It was just that the way Camilla hopped from one man to another seemed to be a rather lonely way of life. Didn't she ever want to spend more than one night at a time with one of her *friends*? Allie didn't think she could have lived quite so carefree. If that's what it was, because she sometimes wondered if Camilla's carefree attitude towards sex and men was hiding something deeper, some fear of being hurt, perhaps.

"And neither do I." Allie closed the cover of her tablet and tucked it under the counter.

"But you can have some fun, can't you? And what's-his-name—"

"Chris."

"Yes, *Chris*, is rather gorgeous!"

Allie nodded. She had a feeling that the more she protested, the harder Camilla would dig her heels in.

The café door opened and Jenny Talbot, the local beautician, strutted in.

"Hi Jenny, thanks for coming." Camilla waved her over to the counter.

"No problem at all. What're we looking for today, ladies?"

Allie straightened up and pushed the strands of hair that had fallen out of her bun behind her ears. Something about glamorous women made her feel a bit inadequate. Possibly because Roger had always pointed out that they looked much better than she did. Allie had felt that way around the delicate-featured Camilla during the early days of their friendship but Camilla had proved to be so down to earth and so funny, that Allie had soon been able to relax around her. But here was the very gorgeous and surgically enhanced Jenny, and Allie couldn't help feeling a bit…

Plain. Underdressed. And awkward.

"Nothing for me, Jenny, thanks, but I want you to give Allie the works!"

"What?" Allie went cold all over. The only time she had any form of beauty treatment was when she'd received one of those gift vouchers for a day spa – which hadn't happened since Mother's Day 2013 – or when she was really desperate for a haircut. And come to think of it, she hadn't had her hair done properly for well over a year. She made do with trimming it herself, usually with a nail scissors, over the bathroom sink. As for any other self-care, well, she might run a razor over the bottom half of her legs if it was hot out and she was wearing a skirt. Although the last time she'd done that in a hurry, she'd used a blunt razor and ended up with red-raw shins. Sometimes personal maintenance was more trouble than it was worth.

Had she let herself go then? In another rebellion against Roger? A man who was no longer here to pass judgement on her looks.

"The works, eh? Be my pleasure. Shall I go up and get everything ready?" Jenny raised her rather large carpetbag in the air and Allie swallowed hard, imagining it contained a range of torture devices.

"Yes, you carry on. I'll help Allie close the café then make sure she finds her way up to you."

Jenny went past the counter and through the short corridor that led off the kitchen. Allie heard her clomping up the stairs in her shiny black platform boots.

"Camilla, this is very kind of you but I don't need any treatments."

Camilla came round the counter and released Allie's hair from its bun, then lifted some strands to the light. "You have lovely hair, Allie, but it's gone a bit brassy. You've been using those home dye kits from the pound shop again haven't you?"

Allie's cheeks warmed. "Well they're a bargain."

"They're okay… but why not have your hair done

properly? If anyone can sort out your colour, it's Jenny. She'll be able to have your tresses back to best in no time, I'm sure."

It would be nice to have her hair lightened a bit. She had noticed that the blonde had turned more yellow after the last home colour and the old washing-up liquid trick hadn't managed to strip the brassy tones away. Sitting in the sunshine with lemon juice on her hair hadn't worked either. It had just led to a burnt scalp followed by weeks of peeling, as what looked like thick flakes of dandruff got stuck in her locks. It was not a good look for anyone, especially not for someone who served food for a living. So she kept her hair clipped back most of the time, hoping the dye would fade.

"Okay. I'll agree to my hair being done. But nothing else."

Camilla lowered into a crouch.

"What're you doing?"

"Checking your legs." Camilla grabbed the hem of one leg of Allie's jeans and pulled it up then ran a finger over her shin. "Yikes!"

"What is it?"

"Yeti."

"No I'm not! It's not that bad." Allie bent over and rolled down the leg of her jeans.

"It really is, you know. When did you last shave? 2002?"

Allie frowned at Camilla. "It doesn't matter because no one is going to see my legs anyway. Besides, it's acceptable now to be hairy."

"One flash of those babies and Chris will run a mile. Nope, sorry, you're being waxed too."

"Oh, Camilla, Chris won't be seeing my legs."

Camilla pouted and Allie sensed she was going to lose

this battle. "Right. I'll have my legs waxed and my hair done and *that is it*!"

Camilla gave her a cheeky wink.

"You know I love you."

Allie couldn't help smiling, but as she took the money from her final customers of the day, then loaded the dishwasher, she had to admit to feeling uneasy. Because Camilla's idea of Allie's best, would probably differ significantly from her own.

"Ouch!" Allie reached out to rub her top lip but Camilla grabbed her hand and stopped her.

"Let it cool down."

"But it stings."

"Don't be such a baby. You've had two kids so doesn't that mean you can handle pain?"

Camilla tutted but Jenny smiled.

"It does hurt like hell but it'll be worth it."

"Will it?" Allie blinked hard to clear the tears. She couldn't believe what Jenny and Camilla had done to her. And although Camilla hadn't actually done anything physically to hurt her, she'd been there every step of the way, encouraging Jenny to *do whatever it takes* and to *ignore Allie's pleas, she'll be grateful afterwards*.

Allie allowed Jenny to direct her from the bed where she'd lain as Jenny stripped her body of hair – except for her bikini line, she'd drawn the line at that. Now she was pushed down the stairs and onto a kitchen chair in the extension, as Jenny wrapped her in a black cape. Allie took a deep breath as Jenny raised her scissors; this was a good thing, but it made her nervous handing over so much power.

Over the next fifteen minutes, she watched as brassy locks fell away to the regular *snip snip* of Jenny's sharp scissors, then gratefully accepted a coffee from Camilla while Jenny mixed up a foul smelling paste in a small black bowl.

"This will get rid of that brassy tone. It will be a bit lighter at first but I can always add in some foils in a week or two if you want some warmer tones."

Allie nodded then Jenny spread the paste onto her hair and scalp, impressed at how efficiently she worked. Jenny's hair fell to her waist in several different shades of grey. The colour would have made Allie look ten years older but on the twenty-seven-year-old Jenny, it was trendy and chic. Allie wondered if it was real and if so, how much belonged to another woman, or man, who'd had it cut away to make some money. She'd recently read a magazine article about how there was money to be made in growing your hair then selling it. Allie wouldn't fancy having someone else's hair woven into her own; she didn't even like touching her own hair once it had been cut, but she could understand how others wouldn't mind. Especially if it made them look as glamorous as Jenny.

"Okay. We need to leave that for a bit, so you can relax. Ooh!" Jenny stepped back and frowned.

Allie watched her carefully; panic flooding her belly like a freezing cold drink.

"Oh dear." Camilla grimaced.

"Some ice will help. Probably just a bit of a reaction to the wax. Don't worry!" Jenny went to the freezer, located the ice cube tray then pressed a few cubes onto a piece of kitchen roll. "Here, hold this above your top lip."

"What's happened?" Allie asked, trying not to breathe too deeply as the smell of the bleach on her hair was making her throat ache.

"Just a bit of swelling." Camilla waved a hand. "It'll go down."

"How much swelling?" Allie asked, pushing to her feet.

Camilla stared at her feet, so Allie went into the downstairs cloakroom that led off the kitchen.

"Argh!" She stared at her reflection. Her hair was pasted to her head making her look like she was wearing a bald cap and the area above her top lip – which used to be quite flat – was now bulging like a magenta moustache. "I can't go anywhere like this!"

"Don't worry. You have an hour or so yet," Jenny called from the kitchen. "It's perfectly normal."

"Normal?" Allie asked. "I look like I've done that stupid lip-enhancing challenge that Jordan got involved in a few years ago."

Camilla appeared in the doorway.

"Oh, yeah. I remember that. His lip was swollen for about two weeks, wasn't it?"

Allie nodded.

"He was in agony. I worried he'd end up with permanent nerve damage. And all to show off to his mates from college when one of them dared him to try for a trout pout."

"In all fairness, Allie, he'd had a few drinks."

"He'd have regretted it if the results had been permanent. Thankfully, it went down."

She prodded her own face tender face and winced.

"Get the ice on it and give it time to work."

"I'm not going if it doesn't."

"You can always wear a scarf." Camilla suggested.

"What all night?" Allie had images of speaking to Chris from behind her silk scarf printed with tiny cupcakes. "How will I eat and drink?"

"You'll manage." Camilla flashed her a guilty smile.

"If this doesn't go down, I will hold you personally responsible."

Camilla grabbed her hand. "Come and have a glass of wine and you'll feel better about it."

"I doubt that but it certainly can't get any worse."

An hour later, Allie was ready. Well, almost. She stood in front of the full-length mirror in her bedroom and surveyed her makeover.

"In all fairness, Jenny, you have worked miracles."

Jenny sat on the edge of the bed and crossed her endless legs. "A job well done, I believe."

"You're gorgeous. Chris'll be all over you."

Allie scowled at her friend.

"Camilla, I do not want him to be all over me. Besides, although the swelling has gone down now, my lip is still very sore."

Allie turned back to the mirror. Her skinny black jeans went well with the sheer grey thigh-length blouse Mandy had bought her for Christmas. Allie had never worn it; not wanting to ruin it after seeing the price tag her daughter had accidentally-on-purpose left attached. But tonight, seemed like a good time to give the blouse an airing. Underneath, she wore the matching grey camisole that clung to her curves and reached just below the hem of the blouse. The layering seemed to help disguise some of her lumps and bumps. She had teamed her outfit with a pair of silver-grey pumps.

Jenny had done her makeup as natural looking as possible, except for smoky eyes that really brought out their blue, and her hair was now a shiny golden mane. When Jenny was cutting it, Allie had thought she was taking lots off, but in reality, she'd merely trimmed the ends and given it some layers. The colour made it appear gently sun kissed and made her think of beaches with palm trees and soft white sand.

"Thank you so much, Jenny."

"My pleasure, Allie. Don't leave it so long next time though. You're an attractive woman and you should pamper yourself."

Camilla let Jenny out then returned to the bedroom, where Allie had now slumped onto the edge of the bed.

"Hey what is it?"

Allie shook her head, unable to speak as Camilla wrapped an arm around her shoulders.

"Tell me."

"It's just… you doing that for me. It's so kind."

"You're one of my best friends. Of course I'd do that for you. I'd do anything for you."

"Thank you." Allie smiled as Camilla squeezed her. "You know, some days I can't believe this is me. That this is my life."

"Why, sweetie?"

Allie met Camilla's bright green eyes.

"Well, I was married with two children. I thought I knew where my life was heading until six years ago."

"Things can change very quickly. None of us know what will happen in an hour let alone in six years."

"I know. Losing Roger so suddenly was such a shock."

"Of course it was."

"I thought he'd always be around."

Camilla nodded. "You were together a long time. And now, here's Chris, back on the scene. But from what you told us the other day, he could have been in Roger's place."

"Perhaps. But it never got that far between us. I mean, a few kisses hardly qualify as a promise of eternal commitment do they?" Allie had told her friends about the way she'd been close to Roger and Chris growing up, and that at one point, it had seemed like she was closer to Chris. But in the end, life had taken an unexpected turn, and she'd ended up as Mrs Jones, not Mrs Monroe. Then Roger's quirks had become exaggerated as he'd grown older and more disappointed with life and other people, and things that had initially drawn Allie to him were no longer so endearing.

"Maybe it meant more to him than you know." Camilla stood up and took Allie's hands then pulled her up.

"Maybe. But I don't think so."

"Well now you have the chance to find out, right?"

Allie gave a brief smile then opened her wardrobe to locate her small black handbag.

"I guess I do."

But after everything that had happened, she couldn't help wondering if she even wanted to know, and if it would be too painful raking up the past.

4

*A*llie gave Camilla a quick hug then opened the car door. She could have walked the five minutes to the pub but Camilla had been worried the breeze would mess up Allie's hair and insisted on driving her.

"Have fun, won't you?" Camilla leaned over and squeezed Allie's hand.

"I hope so. I'm really nervous now."

"Don't be. There's nothing to worry about. But be careful."

"Careful? I've known this man most of my life. He's hardly got serial killer potential."

Camilla laughed. "I didn't mean that kind of careful but you never know someone inside out. So just take care."

"I will."

"Oh!" Camilla rummaged in her pocket. "Before you go, I have something for you."

"You do?" Allie frowned.

"This…" Camilla held out a small square foil packet.

"What's that?"

"Oh come on, Allie, don't tell me you've never seen one before."

"A condom?" Allie's cheeks burned. "I don't need that. I won't be getting up to anything that requires protection tonight."

"Humour me. If you don't take it and the moment arises, you'll be disappointed you didn't. Especially if he's not carrying any."

Allie stared at the offending square of foil and thought about what it meant if she accepted it. But what if she didn't and Camilla was right? She shook her head. There was no way she was sleeping with Chris, gorgeous as he might be. She hadn't slept with a man since Roger – or before for that matter – and couldn't quite imagine that kind of intimacy after so long. Yes, people on movies said it was like riding a bike and that you never forgot, but perhaps you did. Perhaps, for this woman on the brink of middle age, sex was a thing of the past.

"Hey Mum."

"Shit, it's Jordan!"

Camilla snorted then threw the condom at Allie. It landed on her lap just as he stuck his head around the car door, so she quickly stuffed it into her bag.

"Hi, love. Everything okay?"

"Yeah. Just popping home for a shower then I'm off to see Max."

"Oh right?" Allie willed the heat to recede from her cheeks but she was worried that he'd seen the condom. "What're you two going to be doing this evening then?" She'd been so flustered earlier with worrying about meeting up with Chris, that she couldn't remember if Jordan had already told her. During her makeover, he'd been out on his bike, and he hadn't returned before she left.

"Oh, we, um… we're going to be gaming." Was it her imagination or had Jordan's cheeks darkened? But perhaps she was projecting her own discomfort onto her son.

Pull yourself together…

Jordan pushed his hair back from his sweaty forehead and frowned.

"You look really nice, Mum."

"Do I?" Allie sank into her seat.

"Why are you all dressed up?"

"We're off to the pub." Camilla nodded. "Girls' night out."

"Right. Well have fun. I'll see you later." Jordan tapped the car roof then cycled away.

"Camilla." Allie grimaced. "He could have seen that."

"I take it you didn't tell him about your date then?"

"It's not a date—"

Camilla held up a hand. "Whatever. But if it's not, why didn't you tell him you were meeting Chris?"

"I just don't want to worry him. He's been through a lot, you know?"

"We all lose loved ones, Allie. I know Jordan lost his dad but he is all grown up now. You can't protect him from everything forever and surely it's better to be honest. This is hardly a big village and he'll soon hear about your da… *evening out* with Chris from someone."

"I'll tell him later. That I met up with Chris for a meal just to catch up on old times."

"Probably best to be honest with him."

"Right, I'm off."

"Text me later. Unless you're… you know, busy. And if that happens, don't video call me whatever you do." Camilla giggled and Allie shut the car door with a bit more force than was necessary.

Then she hooked her bag over her shoulder, crossed

the road and entered the small garden of The Red Fox. Her heart was pounding, her palms were clammy and her stomach was full of butterflies.

But in spite of all this, she was also a teeny bit excited.

When Allie entered the pub, the aroma of beer and chips greeted her and her stomach rumbled. She hadn't felt hungry all day, but she now realised she needed to eat something.

She scanned the room and spotted Chris at a table in the corner. He raised his pint in greeting.

Damn he looks good.

She tried to push the thought away but it lingered as she took in his salt-and-pepper hair and freshly shaven face. As she approached him, the warmth in his dark eyes made her skin tingle, and when she leaned in to kiss his cheek, her legs weakened at his delicious spicy scent.

"Allie, you look beautiful."

"Thank you. You look pretty good yourself."

He smiled and the corners of his eyes crinkled adorably. The plain black jumper he wore with grey jeans and black boots suggested self-confidence; he didn't feel the need to overdress. She wondered if he'd fretted about what to wear this evening then squashed the idea. Of course he hadn't, he probably hadn't given it any thought at all.

"Well thank *you*. You know," he said as he pulled out a chair for her, "I was actually quite nervous. I had no idea what to put on. I didn't want to look like I hadn't tried yet I didn't want to look like I'd tried too hard."

Allie coughed. Her mouth and throat had dried up. "No way!"

"Yes, way."

She coughed again. Damn her throat was dry.

"Let me get you a drink. I didn't order you one because I wasn't sure what you like these days."

"Pinot Grigio, please."

She hung her bag on the back of her chair and looked around. There were a few regulars and a few unfamiliar faces but The Red Fox offered a delicious menu and cosy atmosphere, so she wasn't surprised to see people she didn't know. Chris had chosen a good table; fairly private and far enough from the bar to avoid being jostled by people carrying trays of drinks.

He returned with a large glass of white and handed it to Allie.

"Thank you."

"My pleasure."

She took a sip of the wine, enjoying the delicate peach fragrance and crisp finish, then placed the glass on the table. She noticed that Chris hadn't bought himself another drink but he still had half a pint left. So he was taking his time, as she intended doing. She'd prefer to stay relatively sober and in control because she didn't know how she'd react to being with him again if alcohol lowered her emotional defences. Although being around him made a defiant part of her feel as if she wouldn't mind losing control, just for once.

"Shall we check the menu?" he asked.

"Yes, please. I'm quite hungry, actually, so I wouldn't mind eating soon."

Allie took the menu he proffered and opened it. But the small black print was blurry and even when she squinted, she couldn't decipher it. She peered over the top of the menu at Chris and he seemed to be reading his with no trouble at all. She couldn't remember him wearing glasses when they were younger but then didn't most people need them at some stage? The optician had told her that it was common to need glasses for reading once you hit forty.

Chris caught her watching him. "Everything okay?"

"Yes. Uh… no. I can't see without my glasses these days."

"Thank goodness for that!" He laughed. "Me neither but I didn't want to put mine on. Vanity, eh?"

"After three?" She swung her bag around and unzipped it.

"I will if you will."

He pulled a small case from the pocket of the suede jacket that hung on the back of his chair, then opened it and held out a pair of square dark-rimmed glasses. "With writing, there's no way I can cope without these. I try not to wear them but it's a losing battle. I might only be forty-four but things start to slide."

Allie rummaged in her tiny bag. When her fingers found her glasses case, she tugged at it, but it was lodged beneath her purse. She tugged again and it loosened and shot out, but as it did, a shiny square of foil came flying out too. Allie watched in horror as it soared through the air then landed in Chris's pint.

He stared at his glass.

Allie stared at his glass.

Then they both started to laugh.

"Oh my god, I'm so sorry."

His face had turned red and he held his stomach as if it hurt. Allie grew hot all over as mortification mingled with amusement.

Bloody Camilla!

"Well," Chris said, when he finally caught his breath, "I didn't expect that to happen."

"Blame my friend, Camilla. She forced it on me in the car earlier and wouldn't take no for an answer." She took hold of his glass and fished out the condom then dried it with a napkin and stuffed it back in her bag.

"I have to admit, I'm disappointed now. I thought my luck was in."

Allie shook her head and removed her glasses from the case then put them on.

"I'm not that kind of girl."

He put his glasses on then gazed at her from behind the lenses, his dark eyes twinkling. "No you're not, Allie. You're a woman now."

Allie raised her menu to hide her face.

What was happening here? What was this strange sensation coursing through her body, making her feel so vibrant and alive?

Whatever it was, she liked it.

An hour and a half later, Allie was thoroughly relaxed. She sat back in her chair and fingered the stem of her wine glass. She'd enjoyed her dinner of vegetarian lasagne and chunky beer-battered chips and was waiting for dessert to arrive. Chris was good company and he made her laugh as he told her stories about people he'd met over the years and about his experience with an overly zealous fan. The woman had followed him everywhere for six months, attending every book signing and reading, before finally deserting him for the next bestseller, a reality TV celebrity who had his autobiography published at twenty-two.

"So you've done well with your books then?"

"I'm no Stephen King but I do all right. My books are a kind of hybrid genre of thriller and horror."

"Are you with just one publisher?"

"Tied in for the next three books because of a rather

generous advance but who knows then? This business is a rollercoaster. One day you're number one, the next..." He shrugged. "It's not for the faint-hearted, that's for sure."

"Have you met lots of famous people?" Allie asked, thinking about her own sheltered existence within the confines of Heatherlea. Yes, she'd had holidays and headed to London for the odd show or night out with the girls, but apart from that, she was either in the café or in bed alone. It didn't bother her at all normally, but she realised that her life probably seemed a bit sheltered and possibly even boring to Chris.

"Some. At book signings and events like the London Book Fair. But at the end of the day, celebs are just people like you and me."

Allie watched as he took a sip of his second pint. His full lips were still so kissable and with his movie star looks, he probably fitted in around beautiful people with ease.

"What about you though, Allie? I noticed how you've deflected my questions so far tonight. Very cleverly but you've done it all the same. What's life been like for you?"

"Oh..." Allie swallowed hard. "There's not much to tell."

Chris leaned forwards and covered her hand with his. His skin was warm and smooth and goosebumps rose on Allie's arms. She met his gaze and her mind went blank.

"Allie, you've been through a hell of a lot. Don't under-estimate that. You lost your husband and brought your kids up alone. I know they're older but you still had to be there for them. You renovated an old cottage and turned it into a successful business. I know I haven't been around but I heard how you were doing from my mother. She said you coped admirably with it all."

"She did?" Allie fought back her surprise. All she'd ever known of Mrs Monroe was as an acid-tongued woman who never seemed to have a good word to say about anyone.

"She did. Mum always told me good things about you, although the rest of the village didn't enjoy such leniency. She said you did yourself proud and encouraged me to come back and see how you were doing. On more than one occasion."

Allie sipped her wine.

"That's not exactly how she came across." She thought of the woman who'd cast icy stares across the post office and been painfully blunt when she'd come into the café.

"My mother was a harsh old bat at times, I know." He sighed.

"Chris, are you okay?"

"I still can't believe she's gone. I mean, I didn't come back all that often but I knew she was here. Harsh as she could be, she was still my mum."

"I know. I'm sorry."

He shrugged then nodded.

"Thanks. I guess it'll just take time to come to terms with it. Like everything in life, right?"

"It's still early days." Allie fought the urge to jump up and hug him. She hated to see his pain.

"She thought very highly of you, Allie. She wanted…" He shook his head.

She realised he was still holding her hand.

"She wanted what?" she asked gently.

"It doesn't matter now."

"It does. Tell me."

"Okay. She wanted me to… for us to… she always thought we should have been together. If she ever seemed at all resentful, it was because of that."

"But why would she have thought that we could have been a couple?"

"She knew how I felt about you."

"How you felt about me?"

He inclined his head.

"After all, that was why I left."

"Oh Chris. I didn't know."

Allie turned her hand over and squeezed his fingers. He'd had feelings for her? All these years had passed and she'd seen Mrs Monroe around the village, completely unaware that Chris's mother had known something she hadn't. As a mother, Allie could understand how Mrs Monroe must have worried about her son. No one wanted their child to be sad and Allie thought she'd struggle to hold back if anyone ever hurt Mandy or Jordan.

But now she wondered. If Mrs Monroe had spoken to her about it, could things have worked out differently? Would it have changed anything?

"It's all in the past now." Chris smiled then gently pulled his hand back. "But tell me more about you and your children. How are they getting on?"

"Mandy's twenty-four now. I can't believe that I have a daughter six years off thirty. That's when you know how quickly time has passed. She's working in London as a publishing intern."

"Brilliant career ahead of her, no doubt."

"I hope so. She's very driven and motivated. Not at all like I was at her age."

"Don't be so down on yourself. You were full of ambition but life kind of got in the way. Besides, I'm full of admiration for you and what you've achieved, especially in light of the circumstances. And things were different when we were young."

"I guess so. I just couldn't envisage leaving Heatherlea after I got pregnant. The world suddenly seemed far too big and scary. Motherhood creates a vulnerability in you that wasn't there before; everything takes on a different slant as you realise what could hold potential danger for your child."

"I didn't really have any intention of leaving myself until… well, things changed."

Allie nodded, suddenly nervous about hearing more and feeling a need to fill the space between them with innocuous conversation. "Then there's Jordan. He's twenty-three now and still living with me. He does some shifts at the café and some odd jobs around the village. He's a good lad."

"Does he have any ambitions?"

Allie scanned Chris's face, wondering for a moment if he thought Jordan should be out in the world by now, following a career in a city office perhaps, but all she found in his eyes was interest.

"Not that I know of. I've tried since he was about four-teen to get him to consider different careers and qualifications but he was never interested. He hated school and couldn't wait to leave. He says he doesn't care about earning lots and that he'll be fine as long as he earns enough to put food in his belly and a roof over his head. Of course, at the moment, he doesn't have to worry about a mortgage or rent, but I like having him around. It would be too quiet without him there. And too tidy." She laughed. "I suppose I could have pushed him harder but I think kids these days have it tough enough. They're all competing to climb the ladder or to be famous and I'm sure it's why depression is on the increase. Pressure makes people miserable and I just want my children to be happy, whatever they're doing. If Jordan is content being so laid-back, then that's fine with me. Perhaps he'll take over the café once I'm too old. Who knows?"

In all honesty, she was glad Jordan was so relaxed

about life. If he'd been more like Roger, she'd have been worried about him. The quest for perfection was one that often ended in disappointment.

"Sounds like you're all doing well." Chris smiled. "I'm sorry I wasn't around after Roger…"

"It's okay. Don't worry about it. I completely understand. You're a busy man."

"I should have come back for the funeral but I just knew how awful it would be."

"It *was* awful. But it's been six years since he passed away and so much has happened since then. He'd have understood why you weren't there." She took another sip of wine, gazing into her glass to avoid meeting Chris's eyes. "I read the newspaper stories about your success and watched that TV interview a few years back."

"Sorry about that." Chris finished his pint.

"Hey it was interesting."

He shook his head.

"I was so uncomfortable in front of the camera."

"You couldn't tell. It's wonderful to see how successful you are. I mean, we went to the same school and were friends when we were younger and look how well you've done. I'm so proud of you." Her breath caught in her throat. Did she have any right to say that?

Chris lowered his eyes and toyed with a cardboard beer mat. He turned it over and ran his finger over the logo at its core.

"I've done all right. I'm comfortable but I'm tired too. It's not easy travelling so many weeks of the year and living out of a suitcase. To be honest, Allie, I think as I get deeper into my forties that I'd like to put down roots."

"Village life appealing to you now?"

"Something like that." He met her eyes and her heart raced at the intensity of his gaze.

"Shall we have another drink? Something to wash our dessert down with?"

"Go on then. But only one more as I've got to be up early for work."

"The burden of being self-employed, eh?"

"Tell me about it."

When Chris went to the bar, Allie took the opportunity to check her mobile. No missed calls but a text from Camilla asking if she'd managed to get a kiss yet. She shook her head then stuffed her mobile back in her bag without replying. There'd be no kissing or any other shenanigans this evening.

Or any evening, for that matter.

5

"So that's one latte, one pot of Earl Grey and two scones with cream and jam?" Allie hovered the pencil over her small notebook.

"Yes please." The blonde woman nodded at Allie then resumed her conversation with the older woman, who Allie guessed was probably her mother. The resemblance between them was too strong for there to be no connection.

In the kitchen, she got two china plates from the cupboard then took two freshly baked lemonade scones from the wire rack. Next to each scone she put a small white ramekin full of thick clotted cream and an identical one full of homemade strawberry jam. Last year she'd had fabulous crops of strawberries and raspberries in her back garden and had enjoyed turning them into delicious preserves to use in the café.

She carried the plates to the counter then set about making the latte and the Earl Grey. Everything was automatic now; she'd developed her routines and enjoyed the comfort that came from them. From baking to serving to making conversation with the customers, running the café was everything Allie had hoped it would be and more. It kept her busy, busier than she could have imagined, and that had filled the gap in her life.

Until now.

Seeing Chris again had made her realise that she used to have something that she no longer had. In fact, she hadn't had it in quite some time, and that thought gave her a sudden surge of disquiet. She had so much to be grateful for.

But…

She was lonely.

And not for just any company, but for the man she'd grown up with, a friend who knew her well and whom she shared so many memories with. She missed Roger in some ways, yes – it was inevitable, even with things being as they had at the end – but she couldn't get him back. However, Chris was here, alive and well, and he'd told her he left because of his feelings for her. Was it possible that he still had some of those feelings? Or was that too much to hope for? After all, she didn't even know if he was involved with someone. It was a question she'd been too afraid to ask last night, even when he'd walked her back to the cottage and insisted on seeing her inside. He hadn't come past the threshold, though, just watched as she'd shut the door then told her through the letterbox to make sure she locked it properly. That had made her laugh, especially when he'd stuck his finger through and wiggled it as he said goodnight.

She'd gone to bed with a smile on her face and a sense of lightness in her heart. Feeling like a teenager all over again.

"Mum?"

She blinked, coming back to reality with a jolt.

"I asked if those scones are going to blondie younger and blondie older."

"Yes they are. And Jordan please don't refer to our customers by their hair colour. They might be offended if they overhear you."

"Well what else should I call them?"

"The two ladies? Or just use the table number."

He grinned at her.

"But hair colour's much more fun."

Allie shook her head.

"Yes, take the scones over then come back for the drinks."

Jordan delivered the scones and drinks then joined her behind the counter.

"Did you have a good time last night, Mum?"

She met his blue eyes.

"Yes, I did."

"I saw Camilla driving away."

Allie froze. What should she do? Confess?

"She did go home early. She thought she had a migraine coming on."

"Oh." He shrugged. "Shame. As long as you had fun."

"I did."

"Mum?"

"Yes, darling."

"I need to tell you something and I never seem to be able to find the right time."

"Right…" A thousand worries shot through Allie's mind. Was he ill? Was he leaving Heatherlea? Had he found out about his father – the thing she'd never wanted him to know? Was he in trouble or had he got someone else in trouble? She looked at his sun-kissed hair and the spattering of freckles over his nose and cheeks. He was a man now but in so many ways, he was still her baby boy and always would be.

"Don't look so worried, Mum. I haven't done anything wrong. It's about me and… and Max. See—"

"Allie!" Camilla bounded across the café.

"Hi Camilla, I didn't see you arrive."

"I got my heel stuck in the welcome mat outside, so it took me a while to free myself. Anyway, Allie, I—"

"One moment." Allie held up a hand to her friend. "What was it you wanted to tell me, Jordan?"

He opened his mouth then closed it again and shook his head. "It doesn't matter, Mum. We can talk about it tonight."

"Okay, sweetheart. As long as you're sure it can wait."

"I'll just see if blondie… I mean the ladies at table number five want anything else." As he went over to the table and turned on his youthful charm, Allie hoped he was all right; that whatever it was that he wanted to tell her could wait. She'd spent twenty-three years trying to protect and nurture him; keeping him safe as he crossed the road, as he used the internet, as he negotiated his way through life. She would do anything for him and Mandy, anything at all.

"Allie, I know you've been ignoring my calls and text messages but I want all the gossip from last night. Was it a passionate reunion? Did he have to purchase more… protection from the pub toilets? Did you rediscover your sex drive after—"

"Stop!"

"What?"

"That's enough. You are incorrigible, Camilla. Nothing happened."

"What? Nothing?" Camilla's mouth sagged open.

"Well not *nothing*, because we had a really nice time."

55

"Really *nice* time?" Camilla snorted. "Nice?"

"Yes, nice. We chatted and enjoyed a delicious meal then he walked me home."

"I'm disappointed."

"Well don't be."

"But I am. I had high hopes for you, darling."

"I'm happy as I am."

"Whatever!" Camilla waved a hand in the air, her red shellac nails flawless as always.

"Now what can I get you?"

"Some hope."

"Hope?"

"Yes. The hope that you're going to see him again."

"Ah." Allie released a sigh. "Well I am actually. Tomorrow, I'm going round to his mother's house to help him start clearing it out."

"He's selling?"

"I would think so."

"Shame."

"Well that's up to him, isn't it?"

Allie turned away then, to make her friend a cappuccino and to hide her expression from prying eyes. If Chris did sell the house, she would be disappointed too. Because now that he'd returned to Heatherlea, she was starting to realise that she didn't want him to leave.

6

------

*M*rs Monroe's old stone cottage was picture-book pretty in the morning sun as Allie opened the garden gate and walked up the path. Ivy climbed the front of the cottage and primrose yellow roses grew around the front door. The shutters around the windows had recently been painted forget-me-not blue to match the small garden bench. The bushes in the garden had been pruned to perfection and Mrs Monroe could still have been there, alive and well. The wiry old woman had kept her path clear of weeds and washed it down at least three times a week and it showed.

Allie found it hard to accept that she was gone. Death was strange like that, taking people away, people who seemed to have plenty of time left ahead of them.

Just like Roger.

She pushed the thought away as she always did, refusing to allow it to cloud her day.

She used the heavy brass knocker and while she waited, she hoped that she looked okay. She didn't usually dress up on Sundays, unless attending church for a special service like a wedding or Christening, but today she felt particularly underdressed. She'd slung on jeans and an old Guns N' Roses t-shirt with trainers that had seen a few painting sprees. She'd pulled her hair into a bun and the only makeup she'd bothered with was a flick of powder just to take the shine off her nose.

But she wasn't here to look glamorous; she was here to help Chris sort through his mother's things.

The door opened and there he was. He looked at her, then at himself and laughed.

"Twins!" he was wearing a Guns N' Roses t-shirt with jeans too, but his feet were bare.

"How long have you had that t-shirt?" Allie asked as he stepped back to let her in.

"Probably the same length of time as you. I bet we even bought them at the same concert."

"The old Wembley stadium."

"When we all went on a minibus."

"Wow! That was such a long time ago."

"What would you have been? About sixteen?"

Allie nodded. "Time flies, right?"

"Sure does."

A memory of the hot, sticky summer day returned with a jolt. Allie had been so young, high on life and full of youthful anticipation. Her relationship with Roger had still been new and exciting in the way that only unconsummated teenage love can be. She'd been flattered that handsome, older Roger, already at university, had been interested in her when he could have chosen a girl of his own age. She'd also been so very naïve.

"Anyway, where do you want to start today?"

His face fell.

"What is it?"

"You are not going to believe how bad it is here."

"I don't believe it. Your mother was a stickler for cleanliness."

"Nope."

"Nope?" Allie couldn't contain her shock.

"Outside maybe, and in the rooms people would see if they came here, but the front room and upstairs are bloody awful."

"Messy?"

He shook his head.

"Dirty?"

He sighed. "Try both and then some. It appears that my mother was a… hoarder."

"She wasn't!" Allie swallowed back laughter. She didn't want to hurt Chris by seeming to mock his mother but she was so surprised. Mrs Monroe hadn't seemed the type of woman to hoard things. Then again, perhaps people never did. No one ever really knew what was behind closed doors, did they?

"I'll grab some black bags and cardboard boxes that I got from the supermarket and we can sort the rubbish from things that can go to charity."

"Right."

"Go and take a look if you like." He gestured at the front room.

Allie nodded then pushed the door. It creaked open on its hinges and she was immediately overwhelmed by the smell of damp and something rotting. She covered her nose for a moment and swallowed hard. This was evidently not going to be as straightforward as she had first thought, and she was glad that she was here to help Chris. It wouldn't be something she'd want him to have to do alone.

≈

Allie stood on the bare wooden boards and stared at the piles of books, papers, cards, blankets, and plastic bags that were stuffed with bottles and cans. The junk dominated the front room of Mrs Monroe's house. The sun shone through the front window, illuminating the dust motes that floated through the air, and the smell in there was so strong, sweet and cloying, that it was making her feel queasy.

"Pretty bad, huh?" Chris had joined her and he dropped a roll of black plastic bags and two boxes on the floor in front of him. "I think there could be a field-mouse or a dead rat in here somewhere."

She nodded. "Mind if I open the window?"

"Be my guest."

She pushed the window open as far as it would go and took a few gulps of fresh air before turning back to Chris.

"I'm just… stunned."

"Me too. I mean, how didn't I notice how bad things had become?"

Her heart squeezed at the confusion on his face.

"How are you doing?"

"Up and down. I keep expecting her to walk in and offer me a cup of tea."

"That will happen for a while."

"You know, Allie, I've been so busy building my career and travelling from one place to another, immersing myself in my books, that I was oblivious to the fact that my mother was living like this. I'm just so annoyed with myself."

"You weren't to know so don't blame yourself. "

"It's hard not to. Look at this mess… and upstairs is just as bad. Mum used to be so meticulous about everything, even OCD. At one point, this front room was her pride and joy and only ever used for best." He rubbed his eyes and sighed. "If I'm honest, when I did come back, I'd take her out for dinner then bring her home and rush off again, back to my London apartment, or to catch the next flight. I hadn't been in here for ages. Or upstairs. I just wonder how long this had been going on."

"What are the other rooms like?"

"Not so bad. It's like she stuffed it all in here and the spare bedroom. My old room is pretty much the same as when I was living here. A bit like the room of a teenage boy." He gave a wry laugh. "Although her room isn't great. You should see under the bed and in her wardrobe."

"In all honesty, I never noticed anything different about her. She was always well turned out when she came to the café and when I saw her around the village."

"That's good to know. At least she held it together in that way. But knowing that she was saving all this stuff at home makes me sad. She must have been lonely."

Allie chewed her bottom lip as she listened to him. She knew what he meant, because it was sad. Mrs Monroe had seemed outwardly fine, yet she'd been dealing with all this. What on earth had she been saving it for? And Judith Burnley hadn't said anything about it, so evidently hadn't been as good a friend to Chris's mother as she'd made out at the wake.

"Still," Chris said, "no point standing here staring at it. Let's get stuck in. If you want to that is. It stinks in here and I wouldn't blame you if you want to leave."

"Of course I'm not going to leave. I'm happy to help."

They took a bag each then got to work.

Two hours later, Chris stood up and arched his back. "I don't know about you but I'm parched. Fancy a cuppa?"

"I'll make it."

"Thanks. I'll take all this out to the back garden and pile it up. I think I'm going to need to hire a skip."

Allie went through to the rear of the cottage and froze in the kitchen doorway. Beautiful solid oak units lined the walls on both sides, and under the window, which was adorned with a rectangular wooden box full of fresh growing herbs, was an apron-front sink with a vintage style rose-gold tap. Of course, she'd been in Mrs Monroe's house a few times when she was younger, but only in the hallway to wait for Chris, as his mother had once explained that she didn't like other people's children traipsing through her home.

Allie located the kettle then filled it and switched it on. She found mugs in the cupboard under the kettle – behind the bone-china cups and saucers that were evidently Mrs Monroe's preference – and tea bags in the cupboard above. As she waited for the water to boil, she gazed around. The units were good quality and built to last. The grey slate floor tiles were pretty with their uneven hues of orange and blue. The curtains on the window above the sink and the one to the left of the room, that overlooked the garage, were pale blue with tiny white daisies embroidered on them. It was clear that Mrs Monroe had loved her kitchen and kept it immaculate. Unlike other rooms in the house.

She poured water over the tea bags then went to the freestanding silver fridge. There was a fresh container of milk in there, a tub of spreadable butter and a bag of mixed salad leaves but nothing else. She wondered what Chris had eaten for breakfast.

When the tea was ready, she took it through to the front room.

"Just what I need." Chris smiled as he accepted the steaming mug.

"You don't take sugar, do you? I didn't see any in the kitchen."

"No, thanks. Sweet enough already." He winked.

"Chris, did you have anything to eat this morning?"

He nodded. "I had a piece of toast and an apple."

"Aren't you hungry? It's gone eleven and you're quite a big guy." Her cheeks coloured as she realised how that sounded. "Oh. I didn't mean big as in fat. I meant big as in muscular and…" He was grinning at her now and her blush deepened.

"Nothing like a compliment or two to make a man feel good about himself."

"I am such an idiot."

"No you're not. You are as sweet as always. It was one of things I lo… liked so much about you."

Allie swallowed a mouthful of tea. "Look, we've done quite a bit now, so why don't we head over to the café and I can make us some pancakes."

Chris frowned. "Pancakes, eh?"

"With maple syrup."

"And chocolate spread?"

"If you like."

"Now you're talking. Not that I need distracting from this mess but I certainly can be persuaded to leave it for an hour if pancakes are involved. As you said, I have all these muscles and they need feeding." He flexed his left arm and laughed. "Well, not exactly up to bodybuilder standard, but I'm working on them. I mean, I work out when I can as it would be a shame to waste having access to all those hotel gyms."

Allie drained her tea then reached for his mug. "I'll put these in the kitchen and we can head over there."

As she left the room, she hugged herself inwardly. Chris might not have muscles the size of a bodybuilder but he certainly had a very toned physique indeed, and Allie had to admit that she wouldn't have minded watching him work out.

Or helping him work out.

Or working out with him.

Or… she wasn't quite sure what she meant.

Allie ladled batter from the mixing bowl then carefully poured it into the frying pan. As the surface bubbled, she got two plates out of the cupboard then located the thicker maple syrup that she preferred. Chris had asked her what she wanted him to do to help, so she'd asked him to make some drinks.

When the pancake was browned on one side, Allie flipped it. She continued the process until all the batter had been used and each plate was heaped with thick fluffy pancakes, then she poured maple syrup over each pile.

She went through to the café and found Chris sitting on the leather sofa reading a magazine that he must have found on one of the bookshelves. On the table were two steaming mugs of hot chocolate, their surfaces were brimming with whipped cream and chocolate shavings.

"Very nice! You know how to use the machine then?"

"I've watched enough times in enough cafés to master it, yes."

"The hot chocolates look delicious."

"And so do those pancakes."

Allie handed him a plate and watched as he lifted a heaped fork to his mouth. As he chewed, he widened his eyes and moaned.

"Sooooo good, Allie."

"Thank you. And so easy to make."

"You'd make someone a good wife…" He winced. "What a stupid thing to say. God, I'm so sorry."

Allie shook her head.

"Don't be. I was a good wife, I tried really hard to be what Roger wanted."

She pushed a piece of pancake around her plate.

"What do you mean?" He put his fork down and covered her hand with his.

"Oh nothing."

"It's not nothing, Allie. I know you, remember. We were best friends for a long time. You seemed happy with Roger though, and I assumed it would always be that way for you guys."

Allie sipped her hot chocolate, enjoying the silky feel of the sweet drink in her mouth. It was comforting, like a hug in a mug.

"It was good between us for a while. Even after we had the two children, it was still okay. We enjoyed a lot of things together but I don't know… somewhere along the way, something changed. He…" Was she really going to tell someone the truth? If it was going to be anyone, she guessed it should be Chris. "Roger liked things done a certain way. I think it might have had something to do with losing his parents when he did. He had no control over that and it emerged in other ways. The house had to be spotless, the garden had to be tidy, the children had to be well behaved and I had to be… perfect. He had a gardener in twice a week, so the roses were gorgeous and the lawn was up to bowling-green standard, and I did my best to keep the house the way he liked it. But I wasn't perfect and neither were the children. He never let on to them how he felt about their so called imperfections, but he never failed to tell me." She smiled to try to lighten the impact of what she'd just confessed. "I don't know. Maybe my bum was too big or my roots were showing or perhaps he just found that he didn't really love me." The old humiliation swept through her.

"Well that's crazy. I can't understand how he wouldn't have loved you. You're amazing and as for your bottom… well, let's just say I've sneaked a peek and it's looking good."

"You're very kind. But things did change between us and Roger drifted away from me. Or rather, we drifted apart." The full truth was on the tip of her tongue – the details about Roger's final day – and she was about to tell him when he spoke again.

"Some men find it hard with kids around, even their own kids. And with Roger being an only child, like you and me, perhaps he struggled with having more people in his space. Although I often thought that was why the three of us gelled, you know? We three were a bit lonely growing up and there was a kind of affinity between us. But I don't know. Perhaps he felt a bit left out because you were wrapped up in the children? I'm not excusing him. If that was the case, as an adult, he should have tried harder. Not that I should be judging anyone." He gave her a shy smile. "After all, I've shied away from commitment all these years. Never settled down, never moved in with anyone–"

"What? Never?" Allie was surprised by the hope that fluttered in her belly.

"Never."

"But why?"

Chris shrugged.

"After I left, I never found anyone who made me want to get married or procreate. I'm not saying I've lived like a monk, because that would be a lie, but I've kept away from commitment like it was a disease." He shook his head then started tucking into his pancakes.

"So you're not seeing anyone at the moment?"

He swallowed before replying.

"Haven't even dated for about six months."

"Oh." Allie raised her mug and hid her smile behind it. Not that it should matter, of course, whether Chris was dating or not, but she found that she was delighted that he was single. And that he thought her bum looked okay.

All the more reason to relax and enjoy her pancakes. Then she'd go back to Mrs Monroe's house and help Chris to carry on sorting through everything. Now that there was no other woman to worry about, she felt even better than she had done before.

7

*T*he next day, Allie pulled into a parking space at the Meadowsweet Retirement Complex and cut the engine. The drive wasn't too onerous and today had only taken forty-five minutes. Sometimes she wished there was a similar complex closer to Heatherlea, even in the village itself, but at others she was glad of the distance. It meant that she could visit her mum and dad whenever she wished but also didn't feel obliged to visit them every day.

Her parents, both now in their early seventies, had lived in Heatherlea all their lives but following Roger's death, it was as if they'd been struck by a sudden urge to change something and moving out of the village had been their solution. Perhaps they'd even hung around there until they thought she was at the point where she could manage alone, as if they knew she'd do so better after Roger was gone.

Meadowsweet was a modern complex with everything her parents had wanted. Small apartments were built into blocks that led out onto the vast rear lawns with luscious green grass that looked as though it had been painstakingly combed. Her parents had a ground floor apartment with one bedroom, one bathroom and an open plan lounge / kitchen. However, if they didn't feel like cooking, there was a food hall at the centre of the main building. There were also shops, a unisex hairdressers, a swimming pool and sauna, a bar and an onsite doctor and dentist. It was almost futuristic in its self-sufficiency.

Outside were sprawling well-kept gardens, a golf course and tennis courts, so they had no excuse for not keeping fit. There were wardens on call at the complex at all times, so there was always help available should they need it. Allie knew her parents paid a high premium to live there but her father was fond of repeating that they couldn't take their money with them, so he intended to enjoy the good life while he could.

She entered the main building and headed through the warm sunlit hall – that strangely smelt of peaches – to the corridor that led out to the lawns. When she reached her parents' white PVC door, she knocked and waited.

The door swung inwards and her mother stood there in a flowing purple kaftan and green monster-head slippers, smiling broadly as she opened her arms.

"Allie, darling. So good to see you."

"Hi, Mum."

Allie breathed in her mother's familiar rose and patchouli perfume as they hugged.

"Come on in."

Allie automatically followed her mother through to the kitchenette where the kettle was bubbling away. The aromas of freshly baked bread and chicken soup made her stomach grumble.

"Something smells good."

"It's our lunch."

"Wonderful. Where's Dad?"

"Oh he went out for a quick round as he put it. Quick often turns into three hours but who am I to complain? I'm just glad he's making the most of the facilities."

"He does seem happy here."

"He's getting plenty of exercise that's for sure and I'm reaping the rewards." Her mother's hazel eyes sparkled as she giggled.

"Mum!" Allie shook her head. "I don't want to know things like that."

"Don't be such a prude, Allie. How'd you think we conceived you?"

"Yes but I only thought you did it once." Allie winked at her mother.

"We're enjoying it even more now we're older, especially since he doesn't have to waste energy taking care of those ridiculously high-maintenance gardens, believe you me."

Allie nodded, keen to move her mother on from the subject of her sex life. "Yes it must be a huge relief." She'd been sad to see her parents sell her childhood home, but knew it made sense for them.

"How are the new owners?"

Her mother always did this, asked about the people who'd bought her old home as if they moved in just yesterday even though in reality it was just over four years.

"Oh they're doing well, I think. I see them around the village and they sometimes come in the café."

"Good. Such a pleasant couple and they have lovely children, don't they?"

"They do, although two of them are at comprehensive school now and the oldest girl is at university.

"Lovely."

When her mother had made tea, they took their mugs

to the square table in the small dining area and sat opposite each other.

"So what's on your mind, Allie?"

"What?"

"I know you, my darling, and I know there's something troubling you. I can almost hear the cogs whirring."

Allie met her mother's curious eyes.

"You know Mrs Monroe died?"

"Yes." Her mother nodded slowly. "We did consider coming back for the funeral but she wasn't exactly a good friend, so we sent a card to the house instead, thinking Chris would pick it up."

"He did and he asked me to pass on his thanks."

Allie thought back to the previous day when she'd started to help Chris clear out the house. After pancakes at the café, they'd spent another four hours sorting Mrs Monroe's front room. They hadn't even managed to get upstairs.

"Well, I've been spending some time with Chris."

"I see." Allie's mother eyed her over her mug. "And how do you feel about that?"

Allie's skin prickled. Sometimes it was as if her mother could see into her heart and mind.

"It's strange. We used to be so close – me, him and Roger – but that was such a long time ago."

"Time is a matter of perspective, Allie. At my age you understand that more than ever. In my heart, I'm still a girl, but my body tells me otherwise, although yoga is really helping with my flexibility. You know, your father said—"

"Okay, Mum!" Allie held up a hand, not wanting another insight into her parents' bedroom shenanigans.

"Anyway, as I was saying, the years fly by. You and Chris were close and you'll probably find you still have things in common."

Allie gazed into her mug, wishing someone would tell her fortune. At least then she'd know if her recent thoughts and feelings were real, acceptable, normal.

"Allie," her mum said as she took hold of her hand over the table. "You are still young and life has so much to offer you. If you want Chris then go get him."

"But how do I know if I do? I feel silly that I'm like a teenager with a crush whenever he's around, yet I also feel more alive than I have done in years. Since way before Roger died if I'm completely honest."

Her mother nodded. "I know things weren't right in your marriage and your father and I often talked about it. Dad always said you married the wrong one."

"But he never said that to me. Neither did you."

Her mother pressed her lips together.

"It wasn't our place to be quite that blunt. Although, we did try to encourage you not to rush into marriage but you were so set on it. And you had to make your own decisions."

"I just wanted to do the right thing. After I got pregnant and let you down by not becoming the amazing chef I'd said I would become, I didn't want to let you down again. And you and dad have always been so happy. I thought Roger and I could have that too. Roger seemed like the right choice."

"Because he had prospects?"

"He did. He was so handsome and determined and he was the father of my child. I just didn't know that his determination and career drive was due to his desire for perfection in everything."

"And none of us are perfect, Allie. Not me, nor your father, nor our relationship. Every marriage has ups and downs."

"Really?"

72

"Of course. But if you're with the right person for you, then you weather the storms together. However, if someone makes you feel that you're lacking in some way, then they are wrong for you. Now though… Chris is back and you want him, don't you?"

Allie nodded.

"I'm afraid though. That what I'm feeling is just because we're old friends. And because he's… well, Mum, he's gorgeous."

"Take some advice from me, sweetheart. Life is short; time is precious. If you and Chris got together and tried each other on for size, who would lose out?"

Allie took a deep breath then released it slowly.

"No one, I guess."

"But if you don't try to see where this could go… who misses out?"

"I get your point."

"That's my girl."

"Thanks, Mum."

Allie sat at the table, deep in thought, as her mother pottered about preparing dinner. She'd tried to help but her mother had muttered something about too many cooks and insisted that she sat down and relaxed. She mulled over the idea of a possible relationship, or even just a fling with Chris, and both seemed scary, risky. But even scarier was the prospect of him leaving and never having the chance to see if there was still something between them.

An hour later, Allie sat at the table with her parents. As her mother ladled chicken soup into bowls, Allie's mouth watered at the delicious aroma.

"Help yourself." Her mother gestured at a pile of shiny brown pretzels on a side plate.

"Thank you."

"Well, you've done it again, Connie." Allie's father smiled at his wife. "Delicious."

"Allie takes after me, don't you darling?" Her mother sprinkled pepper over her soup. "That's why the café has been so successful."

"I certainly inherited my cookery skills from one of you and I don't think it was Dad." Allie winked at her father to show she was teasing.

"I'll have you know that I make a mean chilli." Her father held out his hands. "I'm just better with the ironing."

"That's true. He can press creases into trousers that I could only dream of achieving." Her mother gently touched his cheek.

"You two! You're still so in love."

Her parents nodded simultaneously.

"Has she told you yet, Bruce?"

Her father raised his eyebrows in question. "There's news?"

"Chris Monroe is back in Heatherlea and they've been spending some time together."

"And how's that going, Allie?" Her father's keen blue eyes fixed on her and she realised what her mother had just done; she was making it impossible for Allie to leave without committing to something regarding Chris. There was no way Allie could lie, or even twist the truth, while under the scrutiny of her retired lawyer father. He could spot a fib or an evasion at twenty paces.

"It's going okay, I guess."

"Now come on, tell him what you told me, Allie."

She repeated the details she'd relayed to her mother earlier, and her father listened carefully.

"I see." He dipped a pretzel into his soup then chewed it thoughtfully.

"Bruce, I think it's time to tell her."

Her father inclined his head. "Allie, we never told you this before because we didn't think there was much point. You made your choice and married Roger and gave us two lovely grandchildren. Mandy rang last night by the way and is full of the joys of her job. Lovely to hear her enthusiasm. Anyway, at your wedding reception, while you were busy with Roger attending to your guests, I went out for a cigar." He took another bite of pretzel.

Allie nodded. Her father had given up cigars, as far as she knew, following a bit of a health scare about three years earlier, but she remembered him smoking throughout her childhood and teenage years. The aroma had been almost comforting, something akin to rich loamy soil or a sawmill in the rain, and was one she always associated with him. But she'd been glad when he'd quit because she'd worried about the dangers of smoking.

"Outside the hotel," her father continued, "I found Chris perched on the edge of the stone fountain. And he was in a right old state."

"What was wrong?" Allie's stomach clenched at the thought of him being upset.

"At first, he wouldn't tell me. But after a while, the floodgates just opened. He was very drunk or I don't think he'd have told me at all."

"What did he say?"

"That he was in love with you and that at one point he thought you would get together but something happened and it broke his heart."

"Wow." She stared at her soup, her appetite fading.

"I know he was young. You all were. But he loved you, Allie. And you know we liked Roger but Chris just seemed... more suitable for you. Now I'm not one to judge the romantic decisions of others, and I've been very lucky to have your mother, but I think you might have ended up with the wrong man."

Allie stared at her father and felt her mouth drop slowly open.

"Allie!" He held up his hands so his palms were facing her. "Don't look at me like that. You and Roger had fabulous kids and a long time together but we know something went wrong towards the… end."

"We could tell it wasn't working between you, darling," her mother added.

"How? I barely admitted it to myself until afterwards." She'd never told her parents everything but now they were telling her they had suspicions. Not voicing the truth about Roger's idealism or his final moments had been a way of keeping it from becoming a painful reality. Or so she'd hoped. But the truth had a way of outing itself.

"Chris really loved you. I don't know how he feels now, Allie, but I'm sure he will always be a good friend. Possibly more if you rekindle that old spark. Who knows? At least you're both older and wiser, eh?" Her father squeezed her fingers. She gazed at the white hairs on his knuckles and the slight swelling of his joints. Her parents were getting older; she couldn't deny that and they wouldn't always be around. They were good people and like any loving parents, they just wanted to see her happy. Her life was good now; she had the café to focus on, and her children – although they had their own lives and so they should. She knew they'd always love her but they were adults and didn't need her as much as they once had.

It was time now to think about herself and what she wanted. She was entitled to have a fulfilling life of her own too. But did she need a man for that?

No.

Not just any man.

But it was possible that she needed Chris. That she had always needed him.

She covered her mouth and took a shaky breath.

"Allie, do you want to tell us what happened with Roger?" Her mother tilted her head to one side, inviting her to confide in her calm, reassuring way.

"I guess so."

"We love you and are here to support you, whatever you tell us. And we won't be judging anyone. Goodness knows we've been around long enough to know that most people have flaws."

Allie steeled herself.

It was time to say the words she'd kept inside for so long.

In the café the next morning, Allie felt dazed. She went through the motions of making coffee and serving breakfasts then brunches then lunchtime orders, but it was all done on autopilot. Telling her parents about Roger had been difficult but cathartic. It was as if saying it out loud had made it real and when she'd finished she'd broken down, realising that she'd actually been ashamed about what had happened and blamed herself.

Hearing about Chris's drunken confession had also knocked her sideways. She was so fond of him, and knowing how much he'd been hurting all those years ago made her own heart ache. Why hadn't he said anything? Had he tried but she'd been too caught up in the dominant whirlwind that was Roger to listen?

"Penny for them."

She jumped and sloshed coffee over the counter.

"Sorry, I seem to have developed a habit of startling

you." Chris smiled at her, holding her captive with his dark brown eyes. She had an urge to throw herself into his arms and apologise for the pain he'd felt at her wedding. For the pain he'd felt when she'd chosen Roger.

"I was miles away." Allie felt the familiar heat creeping into her cheeks that his presence conjured. She wiped the coffee up then cleaned the bottom of the mug, silently thanking the patron saint of cafés that she hadn't spilt much. It had probably been too full anyway because she'd been so distracted. "I just need to take these over to that couple."

"Of course."

As she passed him, she noticed that he held a carrier bag in one hand and it looked heavy. She gave her customers their drinks then turned back to Chris.

"Take a seat." She gestured at the table nearest the counter. "Can I get you anything?"

"A cold drink would be nice. I've been sorting through everything in Mum's room and it was quite dusty under the bed."

Allie fetched two glasses of lemonade then joined him at the small square table for two.

"What did you find?" She had wanted to help him with clearing the rest of the cottage but she couldn't be there every day as she had the café to run. Jordan had watched it for a few hours when she'd gone to see her parents but she didn't like to leave him alone for too long, though what she thought might happen in her absence, she wasn't quite sure. She worried about a blockage in the coffee machine perhaps or a power cut though they were both things that would cause her problems too, and she suspected that laid-back Jordan would be far calmer in a crisis than she would be.

Chris lifted the carrier bag onto his lap then pulled out a pile of books.

"Are they yours?"

He nodded. "All six of them are the same thriller."

"She had six copies of the same book?"

He shook his head. "They're in different languages. Translated versions."

"She was very proud of you."

His Adam's apple bobbed furiously.

"I… I always sent her copies of my novels but not foreign editions. There's not much point having those unless you speak Italian, Spanish and so on. But she must have ordered them from somewhere."

"How many books did you find altogether?"

He sighed. "Too many to count and I banged my head after pulling these out so I couldn't face carrying on."

"I could come and help you later, or tomorrow, if you like."

His eyes flickered. "That would've been great but I have to catch the train to London this evening and I'll be gone until the weekend."

"Oh." Allie's stomach dropped to the floor.

"I will be back. I just have a few things to sort out at my apartment and with my solicitor."

"Okay." Allie plastered on her brightest smile, determined not to make him feel guilty. "Well if you need anymore help, you know where I am."

"Thank you." He moved his hand closer to hers and gently stroked her thumb. "I know I came back for sad reasons but seeing you again has been amazing."

Allie tried to swallow but there was a painful lump in her throat. Trying to fight how she felt about this man was proving to be a struggle, and finding out what she had yesterday had only made it harder. She'd cared about Chris so much but made a choice all those years ago because she'd thought she knew what she was doing. Roger had seemed to need her more than Chris did. She had also believed, at one point, that Roger loved her. She hadn't thought Chris felt that way about her, hadn't thought he could see her like that.

She'd been wrong.

But here he was, a forty-four-year-old man, with a successful career and a busy life. Time had moved on, and as much as there might be residual feelings between them, surely there was no chance of anything happening? So she needed to get a grip, and showing him that she was his friend would be the best way she could think of to achieve that.

"If you are back on Saturday, there'll be a party. It's a tradition I started when I opened the café, kind of a summer celebration."

"Sounds great. What time?"

"From about seven."

"I'll do my best to be here."

"Now what else have you got in that bag?"

He rolled his eyes. "Embarrassing newspaper clippings."

"Come on then, let's have a look."

"All right but no laughing. I'm just not photogenic at all."

He spread the clippings on the table and they went through them together, laughing and joking in the comfortable way they used to do. And Allie was warmed inside, because even if there was nothing romantic blossoming here, then at least she was getting reacquainted with an old and very dear friend.

8

The rest of the week dragged for Allie, in spite of her efforts to keep busy. It was as if there was something missing from the village, and even though she told herself it was silly and self-indulgent, she couldn't shake the fresh sense of loneliness.

The day Chris left, she'd had her usual Tuesday evening with the girls and they'd soon worked out that something wasn't quite right with her. It had led to reassurances and wine, and by the end of the evening, she'd been smiling again. But it was hard to get him off her mind and part of her worried that he might not return, that being back in London would remind him of why he'd decided to leave Heatherlea in the first place. *That* being her and the fact that she had broken his heart.

Thankfully, Friday was a mad blur of getting everything ready for the party, as Allie confirmed that the local band were able to play, and that everyone who'd replied to the email would be bringing the food they'd selected from the list.

Saturday morning, Allie was up and about early.

Jordan ran things out front in the café, while Allie baked and stirred, chopped and whisked, huffed and puffed.

The August morning was warm and dry, the air sweet and fragrant with the scents of the flowers in her garden. Allie had to wear sunglasses to set up the tables outside because it was so bright, and when she removed the covering from the barbeque, she felt a flip of anticipation in her belly. She loved this time of year and had always celebrated summer with her children, wanting them to appreciate the longer days and to enjoy being outdoors. Life was for living and summer was perfect for making the most of time with family and friends.

They shut up the café at three o'clock, then Allie finished off in the kitchen and checked her list one last time.

She had no idea what time Chris was due back. He'd sent her a text the previous evening just to say hello and to ask what she was doing, but although he'd said he was looking forward to seeing her again, he hadn't said what time he'd return. And she hadn't liked to ask.

Allie had enough time to shower and dress before people started arriving. She hoped Chris would turn up, but if he didn't, then so be it. She had a life to live and she intended to get on with it.

Allie strolled around the front lawn of the café, greeting friends and acquaintances, and encouraging them to help themselves to drinks. Jordan had helped her to set up trestle tables on the flat lawn at the one side of the path. There was a table for soft drinks, one for alcoholic beverages – which was manned by the vicar, who kept a watchful eye on the youngsters to ensure that none of them tried their luck – and one for food contributions.

The first year Allie had held a party like this, she'd done all the catering herself, but over the years, others had brought their own offerings and it was a relief, as it meant Allie didn't have to make quite as much. It was also lovely to enjoy the wonderful variety of food, such as this year's savoury delights including herb, feta and courgette risotto, chicken and ham pies, minted melon and prosciutto salad, stuffed wild mushrooms, lemon sunflower pesto pasta and olive and rosemary bread.

The desserts on offer this year were coconut panna cotta with strawberry gel, swirled meringues with blue-berry sauce, orange and ginger ricotta tart and raspberry mojito cupcakes. Everything looked delicious and in spite of her apprehension that Chris might not make an appear-ance, Allie felt a flicker of hunger as she eyed the feast before her.

The local band set up in the corner of the garden close to the café, so that they had access to power cables. Jordan had laced fairy lights between the branches of the trees and looped them around the shutters on the café windows for when the afternoon light faded. The braziers were also ready to be lit and every table had a colourful glass tealight holder at the centre, which held a citronella candle to keep the bugs at bay.

Camilla appeared at Allie's side, wearing a white cotton maxi-dress printed with tiny rosebuds. Her black hair was freshly cut, her eyes were lined with black kohl and her lips painted a glossy red to match her nails. Allie noticed, as she always did, how stunning her friend actually was. Camilla pressed a glass of mimosa into Allie's hand.

"Here. This'll help you relax."

"Thank you."

"How're you feeling?"

"Good, actually. I love this party. It just makes the summer feel extra special."

"It does. But I meant how're you feeling about Chris?"

Allie shrugged. "Nothing to feel really."

"Oh come on, Allie. That's not what you said on Tuesday."

"I know. Sorry. I'm all right, I guess. Really hoping he'll turn up but resigned to the fact that he might not."

Camilla rubbed Allie's shoulder.

"He'll come. I have a good feeling about it."

Erica Connelly, the singer of the band, tapped the microphone.

"Hellooooo, Heatherlea! Great to be here and to see you all looking so well. As usual, big thanks go to the fabulous Allie Jones for organizing our celebration of summer bash!"

There were some cheers and whistles from the gathering. Allie waved a hand self-consciously, not wanting all the attention to be focused on her.

"And thanks, as well, to every one of you who brought food and drink. I cannot wait to try out the raspberry mojito cupcakes, so make sure you leave me one. Pretty please?" She smiled and offered a thumbs up. "So let's kick this party off with a little number we wrote ourselves."

The band launched into a song and some of the villagers were soon bopping around on the lawn.

"Coming for a dance?" Camilla asked.

"Not just yet. I want to say hello to a few people."

"Okay. But no mooning around waiting for you-know-who." Camilla headed towards the dancers and Allie went to the table where Dawn sat with her husband, Rick. They were a handsome couple with two beautiful children who were currently running around with their friends, safe in the front garden of the café.

"Evening." She took a seat next to Dawn.

"Hey you." Dawn smiled at her but Allie noticed that she didn't look well.

"How're you feeling?"

"I've felt better."

"Morning sickness?"

Dawn nodded.

"Since I found out, it's become a hundred times worse. I'm sure it wasn't this bad with the first two."

"Perhaps it's because you're tired? I mean, you have got two young children to look after already, so you're probably not getting as much rest this time around."

Dawn glanced at Rick and he shifted in his chair.

"It's difficult with Rick working such long hours." She bit her bottom lip as if preventing herself from saying more.

"She'll be all right. It's just early days." He slid an arm around Dawn's shoulders. "The sickness usually disappears around fourteen weeks then she'll return to her usual superwoman self."

Allie swallowed a response. She wondered if Rick was helping out enough at home, if he did his fair share? If he was working long hours, it meant that Dawn would be spending a lot of time home alone. Allie knew from personal experience that being a mum wasn't easy, especially when you felt under the weather.

"Excuse me a moment." Rick got up.

"Look, Dawn, if there's anything I can do, just let me know. I can have the kids for you so you can get some rest or I'll come over and cook you all dinner."

Dawn smiled.

"Thank you, Allie, you're a star. I'm sure I'll be fine. It's just a bit of a shock still. And Rick's right, I do get over the morning sickness after the three-month point, so not long to go!"

"You're that far along then?"

"About nine weeks."

"Wow!"

"I know. I missed all the usual signs because I was so busy." Dawn shook her head. "But what can you do? It's happened, so now I just have to deal with it."

"Well you both have to… deal with it. Not just you."

Allie hoped that Dawn would soon feel more positive about the pregnancy and that it wasn't just something to *deal with*, or she'd have a difficult few months ahead.

"You're right. I think Rick's just a bit shocked too."

Allie watched Dawn's husband as he accepted a bottle of beer from the vicar. Rick had a successful city career in investment banking. Dawn had met him at university in Northampton and when she'd returned to Heatherlea, he'd come along too. Dawn had conceived Laura, who was now eight, at twenty-five and James had followed two years later. Dawn had given up her teaching post when she was pregnant with James because she'd been struggling to juggle everything. She'd insisted she was happy with that. For a while. But now… Allie wondered if that was still the case. And she wondered if Rick was using his job as an excuse not to be around more.

But, she reminded herself, it wasn't her business. Dawn was her friend and she'd be there for her but she had no right to interfere.

"Isn't that Chris?" Dawn pointed at the gate to the café garden.

Allie's stomach flipped. "So it is."

"Well go on then." Dawn grinned.

"Go on what?"

"Go say hello. I know you're desperate to see him."

"There's some peppermint cordial inside. I'll get you a glass. It will help with the nausea." Allie swallowed her desire to rush over to Chris. She had to stay calm and in control. She'd get Dawn a drink first. Otherwise, she was going to seem far too keen, and she was so glad he'd turned up that she might just wrap herself around him.

And that would be way too embarrassing.

She headed into the café and located the peppermint cordial behind the counter. She poured some into a glass, annoyed that her hand was trembling, then topped it up with bottled water.

The doorway to the café darkened and when she looked up, she almost cheered.

"Allie!" Chris crossed the floor in three long strides.

"Oh hello…" Her heart fluttered.

"It's so good to see you." He opened his arms then leaned over the counter and kissed her cheek. His spicy scent washed over her and she wobbled on her feet.

"Good to see you too. I wasn't sure what time you'd be back."

"I missed the damned train I'd intended to catch but thankfully made the next one. Then there was a delay." He shook his head as if shocked at his choice of transport. "But I couldn't wait to get back."

"You couldn't?" She gazed at his face, appreciating the familiar contours, the deep dark brown of his eyes and his kissable lips that were smiling at her right now.

"Of course not. It felt like weeks, not days, that I was away." He paused as if realising how frank he'd just been. "It looks amazing outside. Did you do all that?"

"I had some help. It's a community thing, most people who attend bring something to eat or drink, however small."

"Great band too."

"Yes, all locally grown." Allie laughed. "They do some of their own tunes but also some covers."

Chris raised his eyebrows. "Do they take requests?"

"I believe they do."

He nodded. "Good to know." He looked at the glass of green liquid she was holding. "What on earth is that?"

"Peppermint cordial. For nausea."

He frowned. "Aren't you feeling well?"

"I'm fine." *Now you're back.* "It's for my friend Dawn to help with her morning sickness."

"Better get it out to her then."

"Yes."

"I'll come with you."

They went outside and Allie took the drink to Dawn, then introduced Chris to Rick. The two men shook hands and exchanged pleasantries.

"So you're Chris Monroe, the author?" Rick asked.

"The one and only." Chris winked at Allie to show he was teasing.

"Wow, great to meet you. I've read most of your books."

"Really?" Chris asked.

"Absolutely brilliant stories. Um… while you're here, if you ever want some financial advice, about investment and so on, I'd be happy to have a chat. How about I give you my card?"

"Sure." Chris accepted Rick's business card.

Dawn rolled her eyes at Allie. "Always on duty."

"Well I have a growing family to provide for." Rick gently patted Dawn's belly.

"Thanks for this." Dawn raised her glass to Allie. "It's very refreshing, even if it does look like pond water."

"There's plenty left inside if you want more. In fact, you can take the bottle home with you."

"Thanks, Allie."

The late afternoon turned into evening and time passed quickly, as food was eaten, song requests were played and the amber-streaked sky turned indigo. Jordan switched the fairy lights on, giving the garden a magical quality. Allie went inside to get her cardigan, and when she came back out, she saw Chris speaking to Jason Robins, the lead guitarist of the band. Jason was nodding, his long blond ponytail hanging over one shoulder and his round glasses – that always made Allie think of John Lennon – perched on his aquiline nose. Allie had known Jason since he was at primary school with Mandy, and although he was a year older than Jordan, the young men were good friends.

Allie stood back and watched the party of people in her café garden with a sense of pride. After she lost Roger, even before she lost him, she'd never have imagined she could organise something like this, let alone do it year after year. Her confidence had been so eroded that she'd barely believed she could iron a shirt to a satisfactory standard. But recent years had gradually strengthened her self-belief. Organising this party gave her a sense of achievement and she found great satisfaction in doing things for others and in bringing people together. With modern life being so busy and such a struggle at times, having a sense of community was important, and for her, The Cosy Cottage Café was the heart of that community. She knew it wouldn't be the same for everyone, but she hoped that the people of Heatherlea did see the café as somewhere they could go to relax, to seek comfort and enjoy good food, a drink and a warm welcome. Special occasions such as this one offered her the opportunity to cement friendships old and new and to bring new people into Heatherlea.

New-old people, even.

Like Chris.

Who was walking towards her right now, a smile playing on his handsome face as he held out his hands.

"Dance with me?"

"I don't dance."

"Nonsense!"

"No, I don't. I'm not graceful enough and I have no sense of rhythm." It was true and one of the reasons she had avoided Camilla's invitation earlier.

"I don't care. You can step all over my toes if you like."

"Oh, Chris, I don't like to be out in front of everyone making a display of myself."

"But you're always in front of people. You run a café, remember."

"That's different. I'm safe behind the counter then. Or hidden in the kitchen. They're roles I'm comfortable in. Dancing is different, it's like… letting go and I'm not very good at that."

He took her hands and laced his fingers through them. "You're a funny one, Allie Jones, that's for sure. Come with me." He led her around the side of the café and beneath the pergola. Fairy lights sparkled amongst the delicate pink flowers of the honeysuckle and its sweet, heady fragrance permeated the air.

From the front lawn, the opening chords of a familiar song rang out.

"Dance with me here," Chris whispered as he gently pulled her close.

Allie's breath caught in her chest as Chris slid his arms around her and rested his hands on her waist. Her hands seemed to have a mind of their own, and they moved up Chris's arms to rest on his shoulders.

They danced together slowly, and the years fell away.

Allie was eighteen again and Chris was twenty. She gazed into his deep, dark eyes and saw what she had seen all those years ago.

Love.

Her heart pounded and she gasped as his arms tightened around her.

"Allie."

"Chris."

"I should have come back before I did."

"Perhaps it wasn't the right time."

"But if I had come sooner, then we could have talked about things. I could have helped you with things after Roger died."

"It doesn't matter now."

"But I wish I had. I just wanted you to know that."

"I'm glad you're here now. I had a journey to travel after losing Roger and I don't regret having to do it alone. I needed some space, to be honest. I've learnt a lot about myself and I know I can be strong, that I can do things I never dreamt of doing before."

"You're wonderful and you've always been wonderful."

He lifted a hand and stroked her cheek, sending heat coursing throughout her body.

Then he lowered his head and kissed her.

His lips were warm and soft.

His body was hard and strong as it pressed against hers.

Allie wrapped her arms tightly around his neck and pulled him closer.

The world spun around them and she became weightless as a long-buried passion flooded through her limbs, awakening sensations at her core that made her shiver with delight.

When Chris finally pulled away, his cheeks were flushed and his eyes sparkled.

"Welcome back," Allie said as her heart filled with happiness.

"It's good to be home."

9

*A*llie floated around the next morning. The sun warmed the floorboards of the cottage and the cats followed her as she moved from room to room. They took turns to rub against her legs and to purr when she stroked them. It was as if they could sense that something was different about their mistress, as if her sudden flush of happiness was something they could share in too.

She did a quick clean around then stripped her bed and put the linen in the washing machine in the small utility room just off the kitchen. She felt energised, renewed, full of anticipation, as if she'd removed her own dustsheets and was ready to face the world again.

When she went back upstairs, she remade the bed and stretched out on the sheets that smelt of strawberry and lily fabric softener. Her entire body tingled as she thought about the party the previous evening and about the kiss under the pergola.

It had been magical and she'd felt as exhilarated as she had all those years ago when he'd kissed her that first time, but without the guilt she'd been burdened with then. The guilt that she'd kissed someone other than Roger and that someone had been their mutual best friend. The first time had been sudden and they'd been slightly drunk. They'd shared a bottle of wine in the pub garden then another before going for a walk to make the most of the warm evening. They'd ended up sitting on a bench in the park, watching as the sun changed the sky from orange to lilac to inky blue.

Made bold with alcohol, Allie had suddenly blurted out her suspicions that Roger was seeing someone else, suspicions that she'd been harbouring for a while. Chris had appeared surprised at first. Roger had been away for the late-summer weekend with friends from university and Allie had suspected he might be seeing a young woman on his course. She'd asked Chris if he knew anything, but he'd pleaded ignorance. Yet, he'd said, because he cared about Allie, if he had known anything, he'd have been compelled to tell her the truth.

Something had come over Allie and she'd turned on the bench and taken Chris's hands. She'd known deep down that things weren't right with Roger but with the naivety of youth and the optimism that burned through, she'd been hopeful that everything would turn out for the best.

But in that moment, as dusk fell, she'd leaned in close to Chris and kissed him. It had been clumsy at first, slightly awkward as the lines between friendship and romance blurred, but passion had soon carried them away and Allie had felt something she'd never felt before. That sense of coming home, yet being free, as if Chris held the answers to all the questions she'd ever wanted to ask.

The next day, following the kiss, Roger had come home to Heatherlea for the rest of the holidays. Somehow, Allie had omitted to tell him about what had happened with

Chris, and life had just continued as before. But Roger had been so affectionate, so full of promises that he would give her a lifetime of happiness. He'd also told her that he needed her, that she was his whole world and he couldn't live without her. Looking back, she realised he must have been feeling guilty about something. But she'd been taken in, told herself that Chris was wilful and independent, that his dreams of being an author might not even be realised and that she wanted what Roger could offer. She'd convinced herself that Roger needed her more than Chris did.

How she regretted that now, but she also knew that if she'd changed the course of their lives back then, she'd have missed out on having Mandy and Jordan, and she would never, ever wish them away. Sometimes things happened as they were meant to, and if you were lucky, it all worked out right in the end.

After all, it seemed that life was giving her a second chance and she was fit to burst with delight.

"Morning Mum." Jordan stood in her doorway, his t-shirt rumpled and his hair sticking out at odd angles.

Allie sat up.

"Morning, angel. How'd you sleep?"

He rubbed his eyes. "Good yeah."

"Where did you go after the party?"

Allie had noticed that her son hadn't come straight home. She'd been very aware of the fact that Chris had hung around long after everyone else had left – as he'd helped her to tidy up and to load the dishwasher – and she had worried that Jordan might have wondered why Chris was there for so long.

"I went to Max's."

"That late?"

Jordan shrugged. "I wasn't tired."

"What time did you come home?" Allie had slept so soundly she hadn't even heard the key in the lock or her son's heavy tread as he crossed the landing.

"Around three."

"I hope Max's mother and father don't mind you being there so late."

"His parents are away at the moment. They're visiting his mother's sister in Birmingham."

"I see. You want some breakfast?"

He nodded.

Twenty minutes later, as they sat in the sunny kitchen eating scrambled eggs, Jordan put down his fork and sighed.

"What is it, love?"

"I need to tell you something."

Allie put her own fork down and wiped her mouth with a napkin. She'd been wondering when he'd tell her what was on his mind but hadn't pushed him in case he wasn't ready.

"I've been trying to tell you for a while now but we always get interrupted by other people or I lose my nerve."

"Jordan, you can tell me anything. You know how much I love you and I'll always support you."

"Well, see, Mum, the thing is…" He took a deep breath. "I'm in love."

Allie's throat tightened and she took his hand.

"That's wonderful. Fabulous news." *And so close to my own!* "But you haven't been seeing anyone. Have you?" Allie thought back over recent weeks, trying to put a face to what Jordan had just told her, but she drew a blank.

"Mum, I'm in love with Max."

Allie thought of the handsome young man who her son spent so much time with. He could have been a model with his tightly curled black hair, smooth dark skin and dazzling amber eyes. He took after his father in that respect and Allie had to admit to having a slight crush on Jerome Wilson when they'd first met. His mother was also beautiful and reminded her of Halle Berry with her effortless elegance and style.

"You love Max?"

"Yes." Jordan watched her carefully and her heart cracked a little.

"And you were worried that this would be difficult to tell me?"

"Well, yes." He bit his lower lip.

"Oh my darling!" She jumped up and went around the table, leaned over and hugged him. "Jordan, I love you so much."

"So you're all right with it?"

"Why on earth wouldn't I be?" She kissed the top of his head.

Things that had previously crossed her mind about her son now fell into place – like he hadn't had a girlfriend since primary school, although she'd just assumed he was shy or hiding his flings from her.

"I'm glad you told me. I have never been anything other than proud of you and Mandy and all I've ever wanted is to see you both happy. If you love Max and he's the one you want, then I am over-the-moon for you."

"I want you to be happy too, Mum," he said, as he looked up at her. "I wish you could find someone to love."

Allie nodded.

"I know, sweetheart. I know."

She would tell him about Chris and soon. But first she needed to know exactly what was happening, because until she knew herself, how could she explain it to her son?

∾

Allie was buttering a toasted teacake in the café the next morning when the door opened and Judith Burnley walked in. Her brown cardigan was buttoned up to the neck and she wore a scarf around her head, in spite of the heat. She closed the door behind her then removed her scarf as she approached the counter.

"Good morning, Allie."

"Morning, Mrs Burnley. And how are you today?" Allie forced the question out, knowing that it would be greeted with a list of at least eight ailments, some of which would undoubtedly make her cringe. Why the older woman thought Allie would want to know about her piles or ingrowing hairs in certain crevices that never saw the light of day, she had no idea.

"I'm not too bad, thank you."

Allie swallowed her surprise.

"Good, glad to hear it. I just need to take this teacake over to table three then I'll be right with you."

Mrs Burnley nodded.

Allie gave her customer, eighty-seven-year-old Fred Bennett, his teacake.

"Would you like anything else, Fred?"

He raised watery grey eyes to meet hers.

"No thank you, my darling. This is just perfect. Unless you're ready to accept my proposal yet?"

"Ah get on with you, Fred. And break the hearts of all the women of Heatherlea? I just couldn't live with myself." She placed a hand over her heart and sighed dramatically.

"There is that, I guess. Maybe next week then." He chuckled at their familiar exchange.

Allie smiled then returned to the counter. Fred was a Monday-morning regular and he always had the same thing: a toasted teacake spread with real butter and a pot of Earl Grey tea. He'd sit at the same table and read the

Sunday Times – that he'd saved from the previous day – from cover to cover, before paying and leaving to take his stroll around the village. Allie admired his energy.

"Right Mrs Burnley, what'll you have?" Allie pulled her small notebook out of her apron pocket and took the pencil from behind her ear.

"One of those frothy coffees and an iced bun, please."

"Of course. If you'd like to take seat, I'll bring them over when they're ready."

"Thank you, dear."

Allie hummed as she made the cappuccino then dusted the top with chocolate. She wondered what coffee Chris liked. Years ago, there hadn't been so much choice available, so it wasn't something she knew about him. It made her realise how much they had to learn about each other, which was exciting but also made her stomach flutter. Would they still like each other as much when they got to know more?

She hadn't seen him yesterday, wanting to spend quality time with Jordan after he'd told her about his feelings for Max, but she'd sent him a text to let him know that she would see him in the week. She was still apprehensive about taking up his time, still aware that he might have other things to do and other people to see. His reply had been sweet and relaxed and he'd told her not to worry, that he was still sorting through his mother's things, and that he'd look forward to seeing her soon. He'd even ended the text with a kiss, so that had to be a good sign, right?

Allie used the tongs to pick up an iced bun that she placed on a small plate then she took it with the coffee over to Mrs Burnley.

"Thank you, Allie, this looks lovely."

"You're very welcome. Let me know if you need anything else."

Allie was about to turn away when Mrs Burnley put a hand on her arm.

"Allie, I just have to tell someone."

Allie met the woman's small hard eyes.

"Tell someone?"

"Yes! What I've seen this morning."

"Okay…" Allie pushed a few stray hairs behind her ears and glanced around the café. Apart from Fred, the only other customers were two delivery-men tucking into cooked breakfasts before heading out to spend the day driving around. She could spare Mrs Burnley five minutes. She pulled out a chair and sat down.

Mrs Burnley took a bite of her iced bun then chewed slowly. Allie waited, fighting the urge to tell her to get a move on.

"This morning, as I was making my way here, a very fancy car shot through the village."

"A fancy car?"

"Yes, dear. It was bright red and very sporty looking."

"Nice." Allie took a deep breath and released it slowly. What on earth this had to do with her or Mrs Burnley, she had no idea.

"It stopped outside the Monroe cottage." She paused and watched Allie, clearly waiting for a reaction.

"Outside Mrs Monroe's place, you say?"

"Well, I guess we should say Chris Monroe's place now, shouldn't we? Seeing as how my dear friend has passed, god rest her soul."

Allie nodded, wondering what was coming next.

"And… the woman who got out of it was just…" Mrs Burnley held out her hands and wiggled her fingers. "A vision of perfection."

Allie's world lurched and she gripped her chair to

steady herself. A woman had gone to Chris's house? A woman who was a vision of perfection?

"Of course, I'm not one to gossip." Mrs Burnley shook her head.

"No, of course not." Allie forced the words out through gritted teeth.

"But this woman knocked on the door and when Chris opened it, he scooped her up in what I can only describe as a passionate embrace."

"Oh." Acid churned in Allie's stomach. Chris had said he wasn't seeing anyone and that he hadn't even had a date in six months but perhaps he'd lied. Men did lie, she knew that from what had happened with Roger and he'd been her husband. Allie had no claim on Chris at all. They'd shared a kiss and some memories, but she didn't even know that much about him anymore. In fact, she only knew the version of him that he'd presented to her.

Dammit! She was a grown woman and she should have known better.

Mrs Burnley finished her bun then took a sip of her coffee before asking, "Who do you think she is?"

Allie wondered if the older woman was torturing her by divulging this information. But why would she? No one knew that Allie and Chris had become close again, except for Allie and Chris. Mrs Burnley was just sharing gossip, as she was wont to do.

"I have no idea. What did…" She knew she shouldn't ask but morbid curiosity overwhelmed her. "What did she look like?"

"Tall and very slim. She was wearing some tight little dress with shiny black heels. Must have been about six foot, I'd say. Flowing dark hair and a tan that couldn't possibly have been real unless she's just come back from the Caribbean. Bet she didn't have any white bits either. Chris was so glad to see her that I predict there'll be a wedding there. Probably on a beach somewhere hot with the sea lapping at their toes." Mrs Burnley smacked her lips then drained her coffee, which left her with a frothy moustache.

"How lovely."

Allie forced herself to get up. She knew she should tell Mrs Burnley about the froth on her top lip but she couldn't summon the energy.

"Can I get you anything else?"

"No thank you, dear. I'm off to the post office next."

No doubt to share your gossip there too.

Allie nodded then took the plate and cup from the table and went to the counter. She rang Mrs Burnley's order through the till then went through to the kitchen and leaned over the sink. Her stomach was rolling so badly, she was afraid she'd throw up and her head throbbed with tension. She took a few steadying breaths, in and out, to the count of ten.

She had been a stupid, stupid fool and let her heart run away with her. Chris was a best-selling author now and she was just Allie Jones, owner of The Cosy Cottage Café – a dumpy, widowed mother on the wrong side of forty. Why would Chris come back and want her when he could have a vision of perfection? Hadn't Roger shown her that perfection was what all men wanted?

She ran the tap then splashed cold water over her face.

Well that was that.

Enough!

Time to get on with the life she'd made for herself. She had no time to waste fantasising about what might have been. She'd shared a kiss with an old friend and it had been nice, very nice in fact, but it meant nothing.

At least not to him.

10

———

*A*llie turned the sign on the door to closed, then locked it. She walked to the window by the sofa to close the blinds and looked out at the garden. The past few weeks had been eventful, and she'd been on a rollercoaster of emotions as well as a journey of self-discovery.

Quite frankly, she was exhausted.

She rested her head against the cool glass for a moment and closed her eyes.

Following Mrs Burnley's news about the vision of perfection in the red sports car, the rest of Allie's day had seen her yoyo between being stern with herself about staying strong and moving on, and fighting a deep sadness that made her cold to her bones and created an ache in her chest that wouldn't go away.

It was all so silly, really. Allie had jumped the gun and allowed herself to feel things about Chris that she had no right feeling. She'd been swept up in nostalgia and what-ifs, and it had ended badly. For her, at least. Apparently, Chris was making plans with a gorgeous raven-haired model.

She exhaled slowly then opened her eyes.

And screeched then staggered backwards.

On the other side of the glass, was a white face, its eyes wide and dark, its mouth stretched in a grin.

"Chris." She covered her chest with her hands and willed her heartbeat to slow down.

What was he doing here?

He pointed at the door.

She unlocked it with trembling hands, wishing she had a valid reason to refuse that wouldn't make her seem completely insane.

"Hey, Allie," he said, as he came inside. "I've been meaning to pop over all day but I didn't expect to find you sleeping against the window."

Allie offered a brief smile. "I just have a headache."

"Poor love." He reached out and placed his palm against her forehead. "You are quite warm. Hope you're not cooking something up."

Allie moved away from his hand. "I'm fine. I'll be fine."

"Okaaayyy."

He followed her to the counter.

"What do you want, Chris?" Her tone was so icy it surprised her.

"I came to see you."

"But why?" She met his brown eyes and saw them fill with confusion.

"Because I wanted to see you. Because I like seeing you."

Allie swallowed a retort about him seeing enough of a six-foot model that he shouldn't need to see her.

"Well you've seen me now."

"Allie, what's wrong? Have I done something?" He ran a hand through his hair and frowned at her. "I'm a bit confused. I thought we were... well, you know." He shrugged.

"I guess we both thought wrong."

She folded her arms over her chest.

Chris shook his head. "I came to tell you that I've got some news. A plan, that is. Can I tell you about it?"

Anger fizzed inside Allie. This man had come back to the village, to her home, and toyed with her affections. He had hurt her pride and wounded her confidence. And he *still* wanted her to be his friend.

"You have a bloody cheek, you know that?" She spat the words at him and he flinched.

"I do?"

"Yes, you do. You come here and make me remember how it used to be and make all these damned feelings resurface then you... you're shagging some black-haired, long-legged..." Allie tried to think of an appropriate term that would convey her anger without making her sound jealous, but nothing came to mind. "Thing!"

"Wait a minute..." He held up his hands. "I'm shagging a black-haired, long-legged what?"

"You know what I mean." Her voice came out strangled. "You were seen this morning. *Snogging* on your doorstep."

She choked on a sob.

The emotions swirling around inside puzzled her. She hadn't felt such anger, fire or need for reassurance in years. Chris might have hurt her but she had to credit him with burning away the numb haze she'd been wading through since Roger died, at least.

"I think someone has misunderstood what they've seen, Allie. That's the problem with village gossip. Can we sit down and talk, please? I feel terribly awkward standing here like this."

Allie watched him carefully. Was it possible that he

wasn't seeing another woman and that Mrs Burnley had been mistaken?

"I guess so." Her voice sounded as if it had come from the bottom of a well. She should give him a chance to explain; she owed him that much.

They sat opposite each other at the table in front of the log burner, and Allie folded her hands on the tabletop.

"Allie, the woman who came to my house today was my literary agent, Audrey Harper."

"Do you always kiss your agent?"

Chris laughed. "She's very tactile but she's like it with everyone. What your source – whoever that was – saw, was probably just her kissing my cheeks in greeting."

"Oh." Allie's cheeks flamed. She'd let herself believe what Mrs Burnley had told her and now she felt like a complete idiot. Not only that, she seemed jealous and irrational, and she had never wanted to be either of those things.

"Yes, *oh*. Audrey came with some good news and that's what I wanted to tell you."

She bit the inside of her cheek, the physical pain nothing compared to the ache deep inside.

"Allie?" He took her hands.

"Yes."

"Can I share my news?"

She nodded.

"Audrey is not just my agent but also a good friend. I told her I want to move back to Heatherlea and that I needed to either sell or rent out my place in London. The mortgage is extortionate and it would be ludicrous to leave it empty. Anyway, she knows someone who wants a city location and is prepared to pay cash for a quick no-chain sale."

"You're selling your apartment? Isn't that a big move to make?"

He squeezed her hands. "It's a move I'm prepared to make because I don't want to risk losing you for a second time. I mean, what if I don't stay in the village, and when I turn my back, someone else comes along and swoops you up? How would I feel then?"

"So you're telling me you're prepared to do all of this because of me?"

"No other reason." He held her gaze, his brown eyes warm and sincere, and she felt him drawing her in, encouraging her to place her trust in him.

Something in her chest shifted a fraction.

"I can't ask you to do that. What if…?" She bit her lip, not wanting to cast doubt on the situation, yet afraid not to voice her fears.

"If it doesn't work between us?"

"Yes," she whispered.

"Why wouldn't it?"

"It's been such a long time and I know I have feelings for you but we've both been through so much and time has passed and we're more set in our ways and—"

"Tell me." He cut her off.

"What?"

"Tell me what's holding you back."

Allie scanned his face, wanting to believe that she could do this; that it would be all right.

"Really?"

"I know something's stopping you letting go, so tell me what it is and we'll put it right together."

Allie took a deep breath then exhaled slowly, clearing her lungs and giving herself a moment to collect her thoughts.

"It's not pleasant to hear and to be honest, I'm afraid it might alter the way you see me."

"Nothing could ever do that." He leaned over and pressed a kiss to each of her palms.

Allie hoped he was right but she wouldn't know until she shared the truth.

11

*D*ivulging the whole truth about Roger was difficult. Allie had never told anyone the truth about the day he died, apart from her parents. It was like admitting to being a failure and she didn't want to see the pity and possibly the understanding in people's eyes.

She wriggled on her chair and pressed her nails into her palms but Chris took her hands again and held them tight. His touch was reassuring, anchoring her to the moment.

"Right. Here goes." She swallowed hard. "Roger and I… well, things weren't as perfect as they might have seemed to an outsider. I told you before that we'd drifted apart and that things weren't that good between us, but I suppose I didn't admit exactly how far."

She scanned his face.

"Anyway, he uh—" Her voice wobbled.

"You can tell me." He squeezed her hands.

"The night he died…" The room swayed and Allie was hit by a wave of nausea. "Look, Chris, I don't want the children to ever find out about this. They lost their dad once and I don't want them to lose him again. Perhaps with them being the age they were, they wouldn't have been that bothered about us splitting up, but I didn't want to risk hurting them."

He shook his head. "This is between you and me. I promise I won't tell a soul."

Allie nodded. "Roger was leaving. I sometimes wonder if he waited until Mandy and Jordan were a bit older, or if he just got to the point where he couldn't take any more. Jordan was at a friend's house and Mandy was already away at university. After he got home from work, he got his bags out of his wardrobe – he'd already packed them you see, something I hadn't known at the time. We'd had a bit of a row that morning but I thought we'd sort it out or ignore it as we usually did. You know, we never cleared the air properly after an argument; it was always left to simmer and nothing was ever really resolved. But when he got his bags out, I was distraught. I begged him to stay. Which was stupid and ridiculous, in light of how things were between us, but I was so afraid." Her cheeks burned with humiliation.

"I'm sorry."

"Not so much about being alone as wondering how I would provide for Mandy and Jordan. How would Mandy manage with university fees and how would I keep a roof over Jordan's head? How could I give them a good life when I didn't have a job? Hadn't had one for years because I'd given up work to keep house. And according to Roger I didn't do that very well. My confidence was shattered."

"Didn't he reassure you at all?"

"He said he'd sort out some money soon, that there was enough in the bank account to cover the month's bills then he'd make sure he put more in. He said he'd see Mandy right, but I didn't know whether to believe him.

About any of it. " Her stomach churned. "I said I'd do anything if he stayed but he just looked disgusted. I grabbed hold of his arm and he shook me off. Then he delivered the ultimate blow."

Chris shook his head. "He didn't hit you, did he?" A muscle in his jaw twitched as if he was holding back his anger.

"No. He wasn't physically violent. But he told me he couldn't bear to spend another night under the same roof as me, that I repulsed him with my... my saggy body and hideous clothes. That I never made an effort anymore, and he hadn't even wanted me that much in the first place. I was horrified, Chris. I didn't realise the full extent of his animosity towards me. Then he told me about her, the woman he was leaving me for. Younger. Slimmer. More suitable for his lifestyle than I'd become. He said she was perfect."

"What an utter bastard. That's totally unforgiveable and if he was around I'd happily give him a piece of my mind."

Allie sighed then rolled her shoulders; keen to dislodge the tension that was building there. She'd managed to keep all this inside for so long by pushing it away and pretending it was all a bad dream.

"So I let go and went back into the house. I heard his tyres screeching as he drove away and that was the last time I saw him. Until... after..."

Chris nodded. "I read the newspaper reports and saw the pictures on the news."

"It was terrible. A horrific motorway pile up. He didn't stand a chance."

"Bloody hell!"

"I assume he was on his way to meet her." She waved a

hand dismissively. "Probably off to a hotel or a night out. Whatever. It doesn't matter really."

"So you never told Mandy and Jordan that Roger was having an affair."

"Nothing at all about it. I just said he was meeting some colleagues that night and that's why he was on the motorway at that time. I guess I hoped they wouldn't find out by any other means. Seeing as how he was dead, there was no point making it even harder for them."

Allie lowered her eyes and gazed at her hands, enveloped within Chris's.

"I think it's amazing that you didn't tell them, that you protected them like that."

Allie shrugged.

"I'm their mum. I'm all they had left. Why would I hurt them?"

"You wouldn't. You have a heart of gold, woman."

"I don't know about that. I've cursed him so many times and burnt a few cakes as I've lost myself in daydreams where I walked out the door before he could. My favourite was one where I didn't cling to his arm and beg him to stay. If I'd only been stronger and not so afraid of failing. My parents have such a happy marriage and I wanted that too. After I got pregnant and I thought I couldn't pursue the career I'd always wanted to, the only thing I could do was try to make a go of it. And I hate that memory of me clinging to him; it's like, why didn't I have any pride?"

"I don't think you did anything that most people wouldn't do. Your world was falling apart and you tried to hold it together. Out of fear for what it meant for your children more than anything. There's no shame in being afraid of change and of losing the life you've had for so long. It's a pretty scary prospect."

"Thank you. I saw her afterwards… the other woman. At the funeral."

"That must have been awkward."

"To say the least. I knew it was her because she was broken. She sobbed all the way through the service then couldn't meet my eye at the graveside. She was beautiful, exactly the type of woman he would have wanted. She's probably gone on to live a very nice life, maybe even has a family now. Hopefully, it's a better life than she'd have had with Roger." She shook her head. "I guess we all have regrets, right?"

"I know I do. But why did you think this would change how I saw you?"

"Well your former best friend was leaving me because I no longer pleased him. It's hardly an advert for how attractive I am, is it? Then there was the total loss of dignity with the clinging to him and the begging."

Chris smiled then and some of the tension in Allie's shoulders loosened. His smile was like the sun when it appeared from behind a cloud: warming, reassuring and extremely welcome.

"You have to give yourself a break. This is all in the past and you are an amazing woman. Look at this business you built all on your own. Look at what a great job you did bringing up your two children. And look at me. I'm back here, still as crazy about you as I was all those years ago."

His expression became serious then and Allie's heart skipped a beat.

"What is it?"

"There's something you should know too. I don't think I ever would have told you but hearing what a bastard Roger was, I think I can share."

"I'm listening."

"You know when we… when we had that time together. That weekend when Roger was away."

"Yes."

"When we—"

"Kissed."

"Yes."

He stroked her hands with his thumbs; it was gentle and soothing.

"Well when Roger came back, I had a word with him."

"You told him?"

"I told him I was concerned about how he was treating you. That I was disgusted with how he had left you worried that he was cheating, that I thought it seemed like he was trying to control you by keeping you feeling insecure. I said that he should let you go if he didn't really want to be with you, and allow you to be happy with a man who could love you as you deserved to be loved."

"Wow…" Allie shifted on her chair. No wonder Roger had turned against Chris if he'd given him a piece of his mind. Roger never liked being told the truth if it went against his own version of himself.

"He accused me of being in love with you and wanting you for myself. At first, I denied it, but he'd been my friend for a long time. He could read me well. So finally, I admitted it."

"You were in love with me?"

He nodded.

"Truly. Madly. Deeply."

"How did he take it?"

"He laughed."

"He laughed?"

"Then he asked me if I thought I was good enough for you. If I thought I stood a chance. I didn't tell him I'd kissed you, I knew that would tip him over the edge."

"He did have a terrible temper."

"When I didn't answer, he leaned in close and told me I would never have you. He said that you were his and he'd make sure you had to marry him."

"Oh god!" Allie gasped as realisation washed over her. "He got me pregnant."

"I don't think it was an accident."

"Nor do I. He told me that night when we… you know… that he'd be careful and I believed him. Stupidly and naively. I should have known better."

"Roger could be very convincing when he wanted to be. And the thing is… growing up, Roger was my friend. But he was always extremely competitive. If I had something, he had to have better. He did want you, I'm not denying that, but knowing that I cared about you made him want you even more."

"And over the years, because you weren't around, that competition wasn't there anymore, which meant that his desire to keep me faded."

"I'm sorry, Allie."

"What do you have to be sorry for?"

"I should have told you sooner or put up a fight for you."

"Things worked out as they did. We can't go back and change anything and regret is a waste of energy."

"Well I'm here now."

"Me too."

"And I don't want to go away again. I want to be with you as I believe I always should have done."

He got up and came around to her then pulled her to her feet.

"I'm afraid, Chris."

He cupped her chin. "Of what?"

"That I'm not very good at this relationship business."

He gazed into her eyes and warmth flooded through her as he gently rubbed his thumb over her lips before kissing her.

"Don't be afraid. We can do this together."

"Really?"

He nodded. "You should have been with me from the start. Now… do you want to try this together? See if we can get it right second-time around?"

She pulled him close and kissed him, letting her answer come from deep within.

12

*A*llie stood on the lawn and surveyed the exterior of the café.

"What do you think, Mum?" Jordan held out his hands. "Pretty good job, huh?"

"It's fantastic. Just perfect for our end-of-summer party."

The trees in the garden and the pergola were draped with strings of fairy lights in the shape of apples and pears and they'd hung colourful bunting from the shutters on the cafe windows.

"Time to get changed, Mum. Before the little guests arrive."

"Come on then." Allie followed Jordan and Max through the café and into the cottage.

Fifteen minutes later, she emerged from her bedroom to find Jordan and Max squashed in the tiny bathroom giggling. She stood in the doorway and smiled as she took in their matching costumes. They both wore Hawaiian shirts and cut off denim shorts and had big moustaches stuck above their mouths.

"You'll terrify the children looking like that."

"I think we look cool, Mum. Kind of like Miami detectives from the 1980s."

"You look pretty cool too, Allie," Max said as he leaned back to look at her better.

"Thanks. I feel a bit daft but it's all for a good cause, right?"

In keeping with the summer theme, Allie was dressed as a bumblebee. Her costume consisted of a black-and-yellow striped dress with a flared black skirt that came to her knees, black cropped leggings and a pair of delicate black wings strapped to her back. She'd pinned her hair up and completed the outfit with a headband complete with antennae.

When they went downstairs, Allie headed into the café kitchen.

"Hello my busy little bee." Chris smiled at her from behind the kitchen island.

"Ha ha!"

He dusted his hands off on his apron then opened his arms.

"Kiss for the chef?"

Allie melted against him as he pressed his lips to hers.

"We'd better stop," she said as she gently pulled away. "Don't want to crush my wings."

"That would never do. I need my honey." He smiled. "Too cheesy?"

"A bit." She grinned.

"I'm just about done here. What do you think?"

"You've done a fabulous job."

Allie eyed the delights that Chris had insisted on making that afternoon. He'd told her to leave him in the kitchen to get on with it, and sent her to get her nails done at Jenny's salon. And she couldn't deny that he had done well. Extremely well. The counters were filled with foil platters of treats including freshly baked finger rolls with a variety of fillings to suit everyone's requirements, cheese and bacon scones, sweet potato, avocado and feta muffins, cupcakes that had been iced so they resembled ladybirds and bees, and mini mixed-berry cheesecakes.

Suddenly her vision blurred.

"Allie, what's wrong?" Chris enveloped her in a hug before the first tear fell.

"It's just… the effort you've gone to. I know you've been practising these recipes for weeks just to get them right and I'm overwhelmed. No one has ever done anything like this for me before. And I know you have a deadline for your next book."

He wiped away the tear with his thumb then kissed her gently.

"I work better under pressure." He smiled. "And perhaps no one has ever done this for you before because no one ever loved you like I do. The past five weeks have been the best of my life. Being back in Heatherlea with you and getting to know you all over again has been incredible."

She shook her head. "I still can't believe it."

"No more doubts or worries, my love. I'm here and I'm here to stay. Now help me get these out to the trestle tables because the children will be arriving soon and I still haven't finished the drinks."

An hour later, Allie stood watching as Jordan and Max guided children – dressed as surfers, princesses, dragons, superheroes and insects – around the garden as they searched for clues as part of the treasure hunt. Her son and his boyfriend had set up a variety of games including bowling – which involved knocking down tins painted with monster faces – and a homemade dragon piñata, which the children would take turns to hit with sticks until the dragon surrendered its sweet treats.

Chris had insisted on being the barman, which meant standing behind the trestle table in his pirate costume. Allie thought his costume of black trousers cut jagged at the knee, white t-shirt, stripy waistcoat, and red bandana perched above a long black wig with a black eyepatch – that he kept lifting up as he served soft drinks to the children and their parents – was fantastic. The most popular drink he'd created was his bloodthirsty pirate punch, a combination of cranberry juice, orange juice and cherryade.

"Hello, Allie." Camilla sauntered along the path, a grin on her pretty face. Just behind her were Dawn and Honey. "What a pretty little bee you are."

Allie accepted her friends' hugs.

"This all looks delightful."

"It's been fabulous so far. The children seem to be having a great time."

"They certainly are burning off a lot of energy and should sleep well tonight," Dawn added as she crossed her fingers and grinned.

"Laura and James are attacking the piñata. Rick's watching them so don't worry." Allie pointed at the tree where Rick was shouting encouragement at James, who was waving a stick at the papier-mâché dragon while his father looked on.

"I was lucky enough to have an afternoon nap. Rick's been making the effort to get home early a few nights a week, so I can rest before dinner." Dawn yawned. "And although I wouldn't have minded another hour, I feel a lot better."

"Yes but that's partly psychological too, isn't it?"

Camilla asked her sister. "Now you know everything's okay with the baby."

"The scan went well?" Allie asked.

Dawn nodded then pulled a small card from her bag. She opened it and inside was a grainy image of a tiny baby.

"Perfect," Allie said. "I'm so happy for you. Do you know if it's a boy or girl?"

"No. We thought we'd wait and enjoy the surprise. I'm just glad it's only one and that it's healthy." She cupped her belly and her expression softened.

"And how are you feeling now?" Honey asked Allie. "Everything seems to be going well with Chris."

Allie nodded. "It is, thank you. Very well."

They'd had to forgo their usual Tuesday evening get-together because of the party. This meant they hadn't had their opportunity to talk yet this week, which was why Allie hadn't seen Dawn's most recent scan picture. However, she had kept them updated about how things with Chris were going. *Slowly* being the word she kept repeating, although deep down, her heart was refusing to listen to reason.

When the grateful parents had taken the children home, and Jordan, Max and Chris had helped Allie to tidy up, she sat at one of the outdoor tables with a glass of red wine and sighed with contentment. Jordan and Max had taken themselves off to the pub, so she was left alone with Chris.

"It's a beautiful evening," he said.

"It is and I had a great time. I put on a goodbye-summer party last year, but it wasn't as much fun."

"Allie, nothing was as much fun for me until I came back to Heatherlea. You are everything I ever wanted."

Allie sipped her wine, enjoying the spicy finish of the good quality Shiraz.

"So where do we go from here?" she asked. "Not that I want to rush things. I mean, you haven't been back long and—"

"I've been wanting to talk to you about that."

"You have?"

"Well now that the cottage has been emptied of my mother's collection, for want of a better word, and had a fresh coat of paint, it's looking pretty good there."

Allie nodded. She'd been round to see how the decorators were getting on and encouraged Chris to keep the kitchen exactly as it was, although she had suggested he put in an island to match the rest of the units. He'd done so with the help of a local carpenter and had proudly shown her just yesterday.

"I was considering selling and buying something else local but I'd like to keep the cottage. It's a good size and with some new furniture upstairs and in the lounge, I think it'll make a great home to spend my twilight years."

Allie snorted. "You're not in your twilight years."

"Not yet but always best to prepare."

"Always."

"There's something missing though." He sipped his wine thoughtfully and gazed upwards as if considering his wording.

"There is?"

"Most definitely."

"What is it?"

"A cat flap."

"A cat flap? Why'd you want one of those you haven't got any ca… oh." Allie bit her lip.

"Exactly." He took her hands. "I want your cats to come and live with me."

She burst into laughter.

"My cats?"

He nodded.

"And you can come along too if you like."

"Chris, that is not the most romantic way to ask me. Although I am glad you removed the eye patch first."

He shook his head then toyed with a few strands from his long black wig.

"This is itching like mad." He pulled it off and rubbed his head. "That's better. I'm teasing about the cats. I just got all embarrassed for a moment there. It's the author in me; I'm terrified of using clichés. Anyway…" He took a deep breath. "I have something for you."

He stood up and pulled something from his trouser pocket.

"Open your hand."

"Why? What is it? Not one of those pirate hooks is it? Or a bottle of rum."

"It's not." He hadn't laughed at her jokes and she realised his expression was serious, earnest.

"Okay then."

She opened her hand and Chris placed something warm and solid onto her palm.

She looked from the silver key to Chris, then back again.

"Allie, I don't feel I'm rushing anything because I've waited my whole life to be with you."

Her heart pounded and blood whooshed through her ears as emotion surged in her chest.

"My home is your home, Allie. I don't want to be without you any longer. I don't want to spend another night away from you. Ever."

"Well we haven't spent many nights apart this past fort-night." Allie flushed as she thought about the times Chris had stayed over when they knew Jordan would be at Max's. Even though Jordan knew about Chris now, she still felt a bit awkward when they were all together. It was as if part of her believed that she shouldn't be dating anyone, let alone a man who'd known his father. But Jordan had insisted when she'd told him, then about thirty times more, that he was happy for her to see Chris, and always would be as long as she was happy. When she'd told Mandy on the phone, unable to get her daughter to commit to a trip home because of what she described as a very busy schedule – including a conference in Brighton for authors and agents – Mandy had gone quiet. Allie's heart had stopped as she waited for her daughter to say something. And she had. Eventually. She'd told Allie that it was great news and asked if Chris was thinking of changing publisher any time soon, which had been her way of letting Allie know that everything was all right between them.

"So let's not spend any more apart then."

Allie turned the key over in her fingers, feeling its weight. It wasn't just a key; it was a symbol of the life she could embark upon now with the man she'd always loved. This was the start of something special. At her age, she'd thought all that was behind her, but here she was with a wonderful second chance. She was still young. Her children were happy, her parents were happy – and delighted that she'd started seeing Chris – and her friends were happy. Everything seemed to be going right for once.

She held the key tight, feeling its reassuring weight.

"Okay."

"Okay?" Chris's eyebrows rose.

"Let's do it. I guess Jordan will be happy to have the extra space above the café now that he has Max. They were talking about finding somewhere together just yesterday, so this will work out well for them too."

Chris pulled her to her feet then swung her round. "You won't regret this, I promise. I'll do everything I can, every day of my life, to make you happy. I love you, Allie Jones."

"And I love you too, Chris."

As he squeezed her tight, Allie peered over his shoulder at The Cosy Cottage Café and smiled. Her life had started over when she'd taken on the café. Chris had returned at a time when she was doing well, when she felt good about herself. And that was important. She'd proved something by setting up her own business; that she was a strong woman with a good head on her shoulders and a good heart. She'd created a small corner of the community where people could go when they needed a break, some sustenance or even just a friendly face.

And now that Chris was here, life would just be even better.

"I think we'd better go tell the cats," Allie said as Chris released her.

"Probably for the best. Wouldn't want those wily sisters finding out from someone else now would we?"

"And one more thing."

He raised his eyebrows.

"When you said you wanted to get some new furniture, you meant old, right?"

"Whatever you want is just perfect. Like you."

Allie held out her hand and Chris took it, then they entered The Cosy Cottage Café together, neither of them ever intending on letting go again.

The End

ALSO BY THIS AUTHOR...

If you enjoyed *Summer at The Cosy Cottage Café*, you might also enjoy *Autumn at The Cosy Cottage Café*

Chapter 1

Dawn Dix-Beaumont dropped the Lego bricks into the large plastic bucket and leaned against the wall. The colour scheme of the playroom had been chosen to create a fun and lively space for their children, but right now, in the early October afternoon sunshine, it was giving her a headache. The yellow walls, the red and blue buckets for toys, the turquoise and purple beanbags, and the green shelves, all seemed to be growing larger as she stood there. Swaying.

Swaying?

She slid down the wall to the floor and pressed her head into her hands. It must be low blood pressure again. She'd suffered with it in both of her previous pregnancies and it had made her feel faint and lethargic. Only it hadn't come on quite so quickly before. This time, however, even though she was only thirty-three, it seemed that her body was not going to take pregnancy lightly.

Thank goodness it was Friday and Rick would be home for the weekend. Since finding out about the pregnancy, she'd tried to rest whenever she could, but it was difficult with two children and a house to run. As well as a rabbit and a guinea pig to take care of.

Shit!

She needed to clean the hutch out before it was time to pick the children up from school. She loved the animals probably more than Laura and James did. It had been Rick's father's idea to get the children pets. He'd said it would encourage them to be responsible and he'd insisted on choosing the rabbit and guinea pig and paying for them. In typical Paul Beaumont fashion, he'd turned up one day with the animals, a hutch, a garden run and all the necessary paraphernalia for looking after the pets.

Dawn had agreed with the concept of pets making the children more responsible, but her initial suspicion that Laura and James would soon tire of the day-to-day care of Wallace and Lulu had been correct, and now it was all down to her. But she didn't mind. She liked coaxing the rabbit and the guinea pig from their hutch, as it gave her a chance to cuddle them both before letting them loose in their run.

Of course, Laura and James did love Wallace and Lulu, although Laura was more interested in maintaining their social media profile than her younger brother was. She regularly took photographs of them on Dawn's mobile phone, which Dawn then helped her to post to the Instagram page that Paul had set up. *Wallace and Lulu's Adventures* was quite popular and received lots of likes, but Dawn also knew that it was a way for Paul to connect with his grandchildren. He was a busy man – even since his retirement – but the convenience of social media meant that he could check in with his grandchildren from the golf course, or the club at the docks where he kept his boat.

Dawn got up slowly, stood still for a moment to ensure that her head was clear, then went through the hallway to the kitchen. She picked up the shed keys and headed out through the back door and into the garden.

The sun was hot. Forecasters had predicted an Indian summer for England, but Dawn suspected that it would probably last a few days then they'd be plunged into Arctic conditions. The good old British weather never failed to keep people on their toes. Gone were the days where she used to pack her summer wardrobe away by September then her winter woollies by April. There was no point now; it was far more sensible to have a range of clothing to hand throughout the year.

She opened the shed and retrieved her box of hutch cleaning supplies, as well as a bag of straw, then carried them across the garden. Lulu, the two-year-old floppy-eared rabbit hopped to the front of the hutch.

"Hello, sweeting." Dawn knelt down and opened the front of the hutch then held out her hand. Lulu's nose twitched as Dawn smoothed her soft smoky-grey fur. "Do you want to stretch your legs?"

She lifted the rabbit carefully out then let her into the large square pen made of wood and wire netting. Lulu hopped about, clearly enjoying the freedom to nibble on the lush green grass of the lawn.

Dawn peered back into the hutch, but guinea pig Wallace had not made an appearance from the sleeping compartment, which wasn't like him. Wallace was quite a greedy little thing and usually greeted Dawn with excited wheeking, especially if she had a carrot for him.

She lifted the latch then gently opened the front of the sleeping compartment.

And there, curled up on the straw, was Wallace.

"Hey little man, don't you want to go for a run?"

He didn't move.

Dawn reached out and stroked his silky white fur carefully, expecting him to jump awake and to see his little nose and whiskers twitching as he greeted her. She gently touched his small brown paws, which made him look like he was wearing socks, then his matching brown ears. There was no response.

His tiny body was cold and stiff.

"Oh no!"

She covered her mouth with her hands as tears blurred her vision.

Poor little Wallace, just two years old like his companion Lulu, had died.

And Dawn had no idea how she was going to break the news to her children.

Or how she would break the news to their grandfather and Wallace's Instagram following.

Dawn opened the door to The Cosy Cottage Café and closed it behind her, making sure that her tote bag was firmly hooked over her arm.

"Hello, Dawnie!" From behind the counter, her close friend Allie Jones, smiled warmly at her.

"Hi." Dawn gave a half-hearted wave then hurried over.

"What's wrong? Are you still feeling queasy, love? I'm sure I have another bottle of peppermint cordial here somewhere. Let me get you a glass."

Dawn shook her head. "No. No time. I have to pick the children up in an hour and something terrible has happened."

"What is it?" Allie took Dawn's hand and squeezed it. "Not the baby?"

"No. The baby's fine. At least I think it is. I mean…" She took a deep breath as a wave of nausea washed over her. "I'm feeling really bad, so I guess that's a sign that the pregnancy hormones are strong."

She instinctively cupped her rounded stomach. She was around seventeen weeks along now, and she felt huge. In fact, Dawn was certain that she hadn't been this size until she was about twenty-five weeks pregnant with her first two. It was getting harder and harder to hide her bump.

"So why are you… upset?" Allie peered at her. "Looks like you need a drink. Sit down and I'll get you one."

"Oh, okay then. Just a quick one. Something cold would be lovely, thanks."

Dawn took a seat on the squishy couch in the corner by the front window and placed her bag on the seat next to her. As she sank into the soft leather, she sighed. If only she could just put her feet up and have a nap. Although it was cool inside the café, the afternoon was hot outside, and her t-shirt was clinging to her back following her short walk to the café.

Allie brought her a glass of bright green liquid.

"Peppermint cordial?"

Allie nodded. "Drink it. You look like you need it."

Dawn nodded and accepted the tall glass. Ice cubes clinked against the side as she raised it to her lips and took a sip.

"That's so good, thank you."

"You're welcome. Now are you going to tell me what's worrying you?" Allie took a seat on the sofa.

Dawn placed her glass on the coffee table in front of them and watched as a bead of condensation trickled down the side.

"I don't know what to do, Allie."

"About what? Is it Rick? Are you two doing okay now?"

Dawn met Allie's bright blue eyes and a lump lodged in her throat. She shook her head.

"No, it's not about us."

Although, if she had the time to talk about it, she would tell Allie that, yes, there were some problems with Rick. Things had improved slightly for a while but over the past week – possibly even longer – for some reason, they seemed to have deteriorated again. But perhaps it was just her. She was, after all, pregnant and exhausted, and it was possible that her imagination was finding issues where in fact there were none.

Perhaps…

"Not really. Things are fine with Rick. I mean… well… they're…" She bit her lip. She didn't have time to air her marital woes right now. "There's something more pressing to deal with." She patted her black tote bag with the white writing *#babyonboard*. Her sister, Camilla, had bought it for her when she'd been pregnant with Laura and Dawn had kept it ever since, using it as a makeshift handbag when the lining of her old one was too sticky with old sweet wrappers and snotty tissues from the children. Rick had bought her new bags for birthdays and Christmases, but they were always designer labels and far too nice to fill with dummies, nappies, wet wipes and all the bits and bobs she'd acquired over the years as a mum of two.

Allie nodded. "And…" She raised her eyebrows.

Dawn opened the bag and stuck her hand inside. She pulled out a small parcel and laid it on her lap.

"You've brought me a gift?" Allie smiled.

"Not exactly."

"Then what is it?"

Dawn passed the parcel to her friend. Allie touched the pink tissue paper then peeled away the Sellotape that held the wrapping together.

"Oh my god! What on earth is that?" Allie grimaced.

"It's Wallace."

"Wallace?"

"Our guinea pig. He's dead."

"I can see that. If he wasn't, I'd be asking you why you've turned him into a bizarre pass-the-parcel."

The door to the café opened and Allie quickly covered her lap with her apron.

"Good afternoon, ladies."

It was Chris, Allie's boyfriend. He came over to their table, pecked Allie on the lips, then sat down on the reclaimed wooden chair opposite them.

"Hi Dawn."

"Hi, Chris."

"You okay there, Allie?" he asked.

"What?" Allie frowned, so Chris gestured at her lap where her apron bulged over Wallace.

"Oh… no." Allie's cheeks flushed. "Dawn brought something to show me."

In spite of the current circumstances, Dawn had to admit that Allie looked really well. Successful author Chris Monroe had returned to the village of Heatherlea that summer for his mother's funeral and decided to stay. His main reason being because he was head-over-heels in love with café owner Allie Jones. Dawn was delighted to see her friend so happy. She'd known Allie for a long time but only become good friends with her in recent years after getting to know her in the café. Allie had been widowed six years ago when her husband was killed in a car accident. But she'd proved to be a strong, resilient woman and had used the life insurance money to set up The Cosy Cottage Café, which was now a very successful business in the pretty Surrey village.

"Something nice?" Chris asked.

"Oh no! Not at all."

Sweat prickled on Dawn's forehead.

"I see. Shall I leave you two alone for a bit?" Chris made to get up but Allie shook her head.

"No, Chris, it's okay. Dawn's guinea pig died and she brought it to show me. Dawn, you need to get it out of here. If anyone sees it… I mean him… I'll have health and safety inspectors all over me." Allie moved her apron then handed the parcel to Dawn.

"Yes, of course."

"How did he die?" Chris asked.

"I don't know." Dawn's lip wobbled.

Allie slid an arm around her and squeezed. "Come on, love, it'll be all right."

"But the children will be devastated. And my father-in-law will be too. I'm sure that Rick's parents already think I don't do a good enough job as a wife and mother and this will just be something else I've failed at."

"I'm sure that's not true, Dawn, especially not where Paul's concerned. Although I know Fenella can be… challenging at times."

Dawn nodded, thinking of how her mother-in-law made her feel.

"Is this the guinea pig with an Instagram page? As in *Wallace and Lulu's Adventures*?" Chris pulled a face.

"Shhhh!" Dawn and Allie shook their heads at him.

"Oh dear… and Allie's right; you can't have a dead animal in here." He glanced around at the customers enjoying their afternoon tea and cakes.

"I know. That's what I just said to her."

"What am I going to do?" Dawn stared at the bundle wrapped in pink tissue paper. "Poor Wallace."

"I have an idea," Allie said as she stood up and beckoned to Chris. "Put him back in your bag for now and let's see what we can do."

Dawn slipped Wallace gently into her tote, then leaned back on the sofa and closed her eyes. She was so, so tired. If she could just have a short nap, then she was sure she'd feel better and everything would fall into place.

Then she'd know what she needed to do…

"Dawn?"

She floated through the warm water, weightless and completely relaxed. It was so nice to be light and free and…

"Dawn, wake up!"

"What?" She shot up through the water to the surface where bubbles popped.

"Dawn, it's three o'clock. Don't you need to get the children from school?"

Allie was leaning over her, with a hand on her arm, and Dawn realised where she was: on the sofa, in the café. She must have fallen asleep.

She rubbed her eyes. "How long was I out?"

"About forty minutes."

"Wow! Sorry."

"Don't worry about it. Do you want me to go and pick Laura and James up?"

"Oh… they won't let you."

"Why not?"

"They've really clamped down on who's allowed to collect the children and I had to list two authorised people, so I could only include me and Rick. My Mum couldn't even be on the list unless I add her as an alternative, and for that I needed to ask special permission from the head teacher."

"Things have really changed since Mandy and Jordan were at school." Allie frowned. "But it's probably a good thing. Shall I come with you, though?"

"No, you have the café to run, and it's Friday, so you'll probably have a teatime rush."

"Chris will help out."

"Where's Jordan today?"

"He's gone to London to spend the weekend with Mandy. She got them theatre tickets and a dinner reservation at a swanky restaurant. Max has gone too."

"How lovely." It would be really nice to get away for the weekend, to enjoy a show and a meal that wasn't interrupted by a child refusing to eat their vegetables or by the other one needing a poo.

"Well as long as you're sure you'll be okay. Anyway, I think I've sorted something out regarding… Wallace."

"Oh!" It all came flooding back then. Poor Wallace. She reached out for her bag and realised it wasn't on the sofa next to her, so she leaned over and spotted it under the coffee table. She pulled it towards her then reached inside but couldn't find the small parcel.

"He's gone!"

"What?" Allie's eyes widened. "How can he be gone?"

Dawn emptied the bag over the seat next to her: tissues, Tampax – that she currently had no need of – two lip balms, half a biscuit, her purse and an old dummy covered in fluff. But no parcel wrapped in pink tissue paper. No Wallace…

She peered under the table again.

But there was no sign of him.

"What am I going to do?"

Dawn watched as Allie tucked her blonde hair behind her ears and looked around the café. There were two customers sitting at the table by the log burner – they hadn't been there when Dawn had arrived – and the table by the other window was now empty, so the elderly women who'd been there earlier had obviously left. But they wouldn't have taken Wallace. Why would they?

"Oh no!" Allie smacked her forehead.

"Oh no?"

"I bet this has something to do with Luna."

"But she moved to Chris's with you, didn't she?" Allie had moved in with her boyfriend recently, taking her two cats Luna and Ebony with her.

"Yes… but she keeps finding her way back here. You know I don't let the cats into the café but Luna has followed Chris back a few times and she did sneak in earlier when the door was open. What if she—"

"Luna has stolen Wallace?" Dawn's heart pounded against her ribs. "What will she do with him?"

Allie grimaced. "She has a strong prey drive. She even toyed with a dead frog that she found on the road once. It was completely flat. I wrestled it off her and threw it over the back fence, a bit like a Frisbee, but she went and found it. *Four times.* So in the end I stuffed it in the bin."

"But this is Wallace!"

"I know. I'm so sorry. However, Chris has popped out to see a man about a guinea pig, so you go and pick the children up and I'll meet you back at yours. And don't say a word about Wallace passing away to Laura and James. As far as they know, he's still alive and well."

Dawn nodded. "Thank you."

"Don't be daft. What're friends for?"

She put her belongings back in her bag, even the fluff covered dummy, then finished her drink and got up. Allie was right; she needed to head over to the school. She hated being late for the children and rarely ever was. The thought of them waiting for her as others went home with their parents and grandparents was too much to bear.

But as she stepped out into the sunshine, her heart jumped, as a piece of pink tissue paper rolled past her on the café lawn like tumbleweed in the Wild West.

Taunting her.

Reminding her that tiny Wallace was missing.

And that the weekend she'd been looking forward to, was not going to work out quite the way she'd planned.

DEAR READER,

Thank you so much for reading *Summer at The Cosy Cottage Café*. I hope you enjoyed reading it as much as I enjoyed writing it.

Did the story make you smile, laugh or even cry? Did you care about the characters? Who do you want to know more about in a future book?

If you can spare five minutes of your time, I would be so grateful if you could leave a short review. Genuine word of mouth helps other readers decide whether to take a trip to The Cosy Cottage Café.

You can find me on Twitter @authorRG and at my Facebook page Rachel Griffiths Author.

With love,
Rachel X

ACKNOWLEDGMENTS

Firstly, thanks to my gorgeous family. Without your love, patience and inspiration, I wouldn't be able to write. I love you so much! XXX

To my author and blogger friends, for your support, advice and encouragement. In particular, I have to thank Alice for telling me that this was possible. You helped me believe that dreams can come true. Also, in no particular order, thanks to Ann, Joanne, Andie, Katie, Kerry, Holly, Sarah, Helen, Heather, Kaisha, Elaine, Laura, Claire, Jessica, Ian, Rachel, Joanne, Rae, Ann, Alison, Clair and Suze – your friendship and support over recent months has meant the world.

Special thanks to the very talented Emma L.J. Byrne at The Felted Badger for the beautiful cover.

To all the bloggers, authors and readers who have interacted with me on social media – and supported me – huge heartfelt thanks. This is a crazy, exciting journey and I'm having a great time with you all!

To everyone who buys and reviews this book, thank you. Without you, there would be no Cosy Cottage Café.

Printed in Great Britain
by Amazon

58097969R00090